YESTERDAY IN
BLOOD AND BONE

ALSO BY MICHAEL BRACKEN

All White Girls
Bad Girls
Canvas Bleeding
Deadly Campaign
Even Roses Bleed
In the Town of Dreams Unborn and Memories Dying
Just in Time for Love
Psi Cops
Tequila Sunrise

EDITED BY MICHAEL BRACKEN

Fedora
Fedora II
Fedora III
Hardbroiled
Sex, Lies, and Private Eyes
Small Crimes

YESTERDAY IN BLOOD AND BONE

MICHAEL BRACKEN

WILDSIDE PRESS

YESTERDAY IN BLOOD AND BONE

An original publication of Wildside Press.

Published by Wildside Press, LLC.
www.wildsidepress.com

For Sharon.
Always.

CONTENTS

ALL MY YESTERDAYS

WHEN I WAS SIX, I spilled a box of instant rice. My father made me pick it up, grain by grain.

The next morning, my father walked barefoot across the kitchen floor. He called me into the kitchen, showed me the grain of rice stuck to the bottom of his big toe, then backhanded me. When I cried, he hit me again.

When I was eight, my father drove my mother to the hospital. While x-raying my mother's broken arm, a nurse asked what had happened. My mother looked at my father, then said that she'd fallen down our basement steps.

Our house doesn't have a basement.

When I was 10, my father drove over my bicycle.

I'd left it in the driveway in my hurry to use the bathroom. When I finally returned, I saw him carefully and deliberately drive over my year-old stingray.

He made me clean up the twisted metal pieces before dinner.

When I was 12, I awoke in the middle of the night to the sound of my father shouting and my mother crying as he hit her.

I stuffed my head under my pillows and tried to sleep.

When I was 14, I called my father a name. He slugged me, knocking me into the living room wall. Then he grabbed my shirt collar and dragged me to his bedroom. He pushed me down on the bed. With one hand he opened the drawer of his nightstand, removing a revolver I had seen only once before. He shoved the barrel into my mouth. Between clenched teeth, he whispered, "Don't you ever call me that again."

Then he pulled the trigger. The hammer snapped down on an empty chamber, but I had already wet my pants.

Last night, I heard my mother screaming again. I tried to stuff pillows around my head like I had done before, but this time I couldn't muffle the sounds. Then I heard a loud thump against the wall and my mother stopped screaming.

This morning, I woke to find my father cooking breakfast. I asked him where mother had gone.

"Out," he said. "Get ready for school."

My father left before I did, earlier then he'd ever left before. I saw him put a shovel in the car.

While gathering my schoolbooks, I glanced into my parents' bedroom. The bedspread had disappeared and the bed remained unmade. My mother never left the bed unmade. My father wouldn't allow it. I stayed home from school and thought about it.

Early this afternoon, I searched through my father's nightstand and found his revolver. I loaded it.

At five o'clock, I moved the lounge chair into the foyer, facing the front door. I sat in the chair and cradled the heavy gun in my lap.

A few minutes ago, I heard the garage door open and my father's car pull in. Within moments, my father will open the front door.

CUTS LIKE A KNIFE

THE SECOND OFFICER stood to my right, just inside the door, while his partner tossed my room. Neither man spoke until my mattress had been up-ended, my bookshelves overturned, my dresser drawers emptied, and the clothes from my only closet dumped onto the floor.

The homicide cop performing the illegal search finally stopped, peeled off skin-tight latex gloves, and slipped them into his pants pocket. Half-moons of sweat stained his armpits, and his shirt tail had worked itself free. He reached back to tuck it in as he crossed the room toward us.

"There's nothing here," Zebrowski told his new partner. A thick stump of a man with closely-cropped hair like steel bristles, Zebrowski still wore a thin, discolored scar along the left side of his jaw where I'd cut him with a pearl-handled switchblade seventeen years earlier. He hadn't been a cop then and I hadn't been a two-time loser.

Zebrowski breathed heavily, stale breath reeking of garlic and onion. When his partner winced at the odor, Zebrowski reached into his pocket for a roll of candy, prized a peppermint free with his thumb and popped it into his mouth. It clicked against his teeth as he spoke.

"There've been complaints," Zebrowski told me. "Your P.O. thinks you're in violation."

I said nothing.

"Got a report you've been consorting with known felons. Word is maybe you've picked up a new blade."

Cutlery had always been my downfall. I'd spent time in juvenile detention after cutting Zebrowski during a scuffle over a girl, and time in Stateville after carving my initials on the chest of a welsher after winning a game of billiards — but I hadn't touched a blade since leaving prison. I said nothing.

"We'll be back."

Zebrowski's latest partner, a thin, ebony-skinned cop I'd never seen before, had remained silent during their entire visit. After Zebrowski retrieved his jacket from where he'd slung it over the doorknob, he shrugged into it and they stepped out of my room. I heard Zebrowski whistling a vaguely familiar country-western tune as I closed the door behind the two cops.

Finally alone, I righted my only chair and sank into it.

A LIGHT TAPPING roused me a few hours later. I pulled the door open to find Nikki standing in the hall, an unopened fifth of Jack Daniel's in one hand and two clean tumblers in the other.

"It's colder than my mother's heart out there," Nikki said. She'd just walked home from work, stopping in her room next door only long enough to shed her coat, and her erect nipples, still constricted from the cold, strained against her tight-fitting white blouse. Her stone-washed jeans could have been tattooed on and her blood-red stiletto heels sliced at the carpet as she pushed her way past me.

Nikki stopped suddenly when she saw the condition of my room. "What happened here?"

I told her.

"They ever going to leave you alone?"

I told her I didn't think so.

I'd first met Nikki when the inch-long black roots on her shoulder-length hair were still blonde and she'd been resident in the room next to mine barely a week. Our relationship had begun with the recognition of our mutual need for companionship and our realization that our past relationships prevented us from ever imagining a future. We smoked together, we drank together, we slept together, and we never voiced the words that both of us longed to hear.

Nikki broke the bottle's seal, poured us each two fingers of Jack, then helped me return everything to its assigned place. Only the wicker waste basket in the bathroom had escaped Zebrowski's methodical mayhem.

"Somebody kicked the carpet loose again," Nikki said as she smoothed the green pile near the dresser. "I thought you asked the super to fix it."

"I have, and he hasn't fixed the running toilet yet, either," I said.

"You just don't know how to handle him."

When my room had been reassembled and all my books reshelved in proper Dewey Decimal order, Nikki knelt on the bed behind me and massaged my shoulders. As I relaxed, she reached around and unbuttoned my rumpled shirt, pushing it down my arms.

"You've kept out of trouble," Nikki whispered. "You have nothing to worry about."

She kissed the back of my neck, her full lips moist against my skin, and I melted back against her, feeling her heavy breasts press against my shoulders. I turned to face her, slid my hands up under her blouse and over her breasts. Her nipples stiffened and pressed against my palms. Then her mouth fastened on mine, our lips parted, and our tongues met.

I'm not sure how we disrobed since I don't remember taking my hands from Nikki's body, but we fucked and drank until the Jack disappeared. Then Nikki and I shared the last cigarette from a crumpled Marlboro soft pack I found on the nightstand. Before long, she fell asleep cradled in my arms, her head on my shoulder and her breath tickling my chest hair. I stared at the whorls of paint on the ceiling until dawn assaulted my room through a gap in the faded curtains, then I slipped from under Nikki and padded into the bathroom.

I carefully poured the contents of the waste basket onto the gray-and-white tile floor. I nudged aside soiled tissues, cardboard toilet paper cores, and junk mail. Under the Publisher's Clearing House sweepstakes offer I found two ticket stubs from the previous evening's Garth Brooks concert, a concert I had not attended.

I didn't touch them. Instead, I used a tissue to push the stubs into a discarded envelope, then left it on the counter while I shaved, showered, and toweled dry. I pulled on the least rumpled clothes I could find in the closet and tucked the envelope containing the two ticket stubs into my pocket. Before I vacated the bathroom, I urinated and flushed.

Nikki snored softly as I pulled the door closed behind me. From the transient hotel where we lived, I headed uptown to the city library.

About halfway to work, I passed a group of indigents huddled around a fire they'd started in a fifty-gallon drum. I joined them for a moment, warming my hands as I dropped the ticket stubs and the envelope into the flames.

I'D LEARNED THE Dewey Decimal system during my incarceration and two weeks after my release I found a part-time job returning books to their shelves in the public library.

No one greeted me when I arrived, perhaps still afraid to make eye contact with the only ex-con they'd ever met. I clocked in, found the returned books cart overflowing, and made my way through the stacks replacing the individual volumes in their proper places.

"Did you see the paper this morning?" A woman's heavy whisper, deep and hoarse from too many cigarettes and not enough estrogen, filtered through the book shelves. "They found a dead woman not two blocks from here."

She received a muffled response from her male companion. I could see her blue rinse beehive and his bald liver-spotted pate through the shelves and I listened a moment longer.

"Stabbed to death," said the woman. "I'm telling you it's not safe to walk the streets alone any more."

"Like you should worry with your face like a truck?"

I returned a heavy volume on general psychiatry to the shelf and then wheeled my cart away. As soon as I had reason to pass through the periodical room, I stopped and examined that morning's newspaper. With the turmoil overseas and all the president's proposed reforms, murder had been bumped from the front page. I finally found the story at the bottom of page three.

A young waitress from the neighborhood had been found stabbed to death in her apartment. There were no signs of forced entry and she still wore the remains of the Garth Brooks T-shirt she'd bought earlier that evening.

Zebrowski and I both knew the dead woman. We'd attended high school with Sharon Stemple's older sister and were both regulars at the diner where she waitressed. From my favorite booth in the back, I had often watched Zebrowski and his former partner hit on Sharon, their comments increasingly lewd and suggestive. Years before I had defended Sharon's older sister against Zebrowski's unwanted advances, but experience had convinced me that I could never again be a knight in shining armor.

THE MORNING QUICKLY disappeared and as I took my coat from the rack at the end of the day, Nikki burst into the library's employee lounge. She collapsed in my arms, crying.

"I killed that cop."

Nikki had run four blocks in the cold and wasn't wearing a coat. We were alone in the room and I held her in my arms. I couldn't tell if her shivering came from cold or from fear. "Zebrowski?"

"I heard someone in your room. I thought you'd come home early."

"And?"

"The door wasn't locked so I went in without knocking," she said. "I wanted to ask you about this." She held up a pearl-handled switch-blade encased in a zip-lock baggie. The bloody blade protruded through the clear plastic. Dried blood covered the handle inside the baggie. "The toilet kept running after you left and the sound woke me. I lifted the lid to reset the stopper and I found this in the tank."

The switchblade wasn't mine. "Why do you think you killed Zebrowski?"

"The cop came out of the bathroom and when he saw me he came at me. I must have panicked and hit the switch on the knife. He stumbled on the loose carpet by your dresser and he fell onto the blade."

I took the switchblade from her hand, admiring its balance. I tried to fold the blade back into the pearl handle, but the plastic bag interfered.

"He wasn't breathing when I left."

"Did anyone see you?"

Nikki shook her head. "I didn't know what to do."

I removed the switchblade from the baggie, folded the blade into the handle, and pocketed it. Then I wadded the blood-spattered baggie into a tiny plastic ball and stuffed it into a trash can.

I wrapped my coat around Nikki's shoulders, then found a crumpled five in my pocket and slipped it into her hand. "Go to the diner and get yourself a cup of coffee."

We walked outside together. She turned left at the corner and headed toward the diner; I walked straight back to the transient hotel, my hands buried in my pockets and my shirt collar turned up against the cold.

Sharon Stemple had been stabbed to death after a Garth Brooks concert and Zebrowski had left me in possession of a bloody switchblade and a pair of concert tickets. I had disposed of the concert tickets, I could dispose of the blade, but it would be impossible to remove Zebrowski from my room.

THE SECOND OFFICER stood to my right, just inside the door, staring at Zebrowski's body. After he carefully accepted the switchblade I removed from my pocket, he slid it into an evidence bag. Then I held my arms out, expecting him to bind my wrists together with the stainless steel handcuffs he carried in the leather holster attached to his belt.

The thin, ebony-skinned cop had watched Zebrowski plant the evidence in my room the night before and I expected him to deny his involvement. Instead, he shook his head slowly, then finally spoke.

"Internal Affairs," he said. "There've been a few improprieties."

He explained what they were.

I FOUND NIKKI at the diner, hunched over a steaming cup of coffee. When I slid into the booth opposite her, she brightened. I reached across the Formica table top and took one of her hands in mine. I'd just come in from the cold and her hand warmed mine.

"Everything'll be okay," I told her. Then I told Nikki what Zebrowski's last partner had told me. Hiding behind his badge, Zebrowski had assaulted a number of women. Although three women had reported him, none had been willing to testify in court. "His ex-partner had covered for Zebrowski," I explained. "That's why his new partner came from Internal Affairs."

"And last night?" Nikki asked.

"Last night things went too far. Zebrowski wasn't on duty when he killed Sharon Stemple, and the officer from Internal Affairs didn't realize why Zebrowski tossed my apartment until this morning." I paused so an anemic teenager with bad skin could take my order for scrambled eggs, toast, and coffee.

"No one knows who killed Zebrowski," I continued, "but my fingerprints are on the switchblade." I'd ensured that by taking the knife from the baggie and handling it repeatedly. "I'll take the rap for it."

Nikki protested. "I can't let you do that."

I squeezed Nikki's hand gently and told her I loved her. Tears seeped from the corners of her eyes.

Outside, snow began falling, silently covering the city.

DOGGING IT

THE THIRD PUNCH laid me flat on my back and Edgar Weinberger stood above me massaging the knuckles of his right hand with the thick fingers of his left.

I stayed on the floor until Weinberger and his two friends left the bar, then Angelou helped me up and into our booth. She dipped the corner of a linen napkin into her ice water, then pressed it against the corner of my mouth, stemming the flow of blood where my lip had been caught between my incisor and Weinberger's right hook.

"I'll be okay," I mumbled through the napkin. I took it from her hand and held it myself.

Angelou settled in the booth across from me. "What was that all about?"

I shrugged. "A difference of opinion."

"Hell of a way to end the discussion."

A waitress interrupted us. "The manager thinks it's about time you settled your bill."

Not a particularly subtle way to ask us to leave, but effective. I dropped a pair of twenties on the table without looking at the check, knowing the tip I'd left was more than generous. Then Angelou and I stood.

"It's another five if you take the napkin," the waitress said.

I wiped my mouth one last time, then dropped the bloody cloth on the table.

Angelou took my elbow and guided me out to her car. Angelou hadn't been working for me back when Weinberger had hired me to find his missing wife, so I told her about it. He'd said his wife had run off with his best friend, but then didn't tell me his best friend's name.

"She disappeared," Weinberger said. "Poof. Gone. Thin air."

"Nobody disappears like that," I told him. "I can find her."

He gave me a photo of his wife and a five hundred dollar retainer.

I started looking the next day, tracking Nannette Weinberger's Social Security number through the State Employment Agency and through a pair of credit bureaus where I had connections. Within forty-eight hours I had a lead. Mrs. Weinberger had a gold card, but the bills weren't sent to her home address. They were sent to a cheap motel in a dingy little town nearly two hundred miles south of the city.

The next morning, I made the drive. When I knocked on the motel room door, a dog barked. Impatient, I knocked again. The dog barked again.

Finally the door opened, but only as far as the safety chain would allow. A slender brunette peered out through the crack. A toy poodle stuck its nose between her legs and looked up at me.

"Let me in, Mrs. Weinberger."

"I'm not —"

"I know who you are, don't bother to lie."

She closed the door, pulled the safety chain free, then reopened it. "So who are you?"

I introduced myself, showed her my license, then pushed my way into the room.

"Your husband said you ran off with his best friend," I said. "What happened, he dump you?"

She shook her head, then introduced me to Maurice. Maurice yipped a greeting. I laughed.

"He's a champion show dog," she explained, "worth a bundle."

"Edgar wants you back."

"He doesn't want me. He wants Maurice."

"So, you holding the dog for ransom?" I asked.

"I don't want anything from my husband, except a divorce. And Maurice. Maurice is the only good thing I took from that marriage." She finally closed the door behind us. Then she offered me a seat and a drink.

"Thanks, Mrs. Weinberger," I said when I accepted the glass she offered a moment later.

"Please, call me Nan," she insisted. "All my friends do."

I'd known her for less than ten minutes. I didn't think I qualified as a friend.

"How'd you find me?" she asked. She sat on the edge of the bed and crossed her legs. Her skirt slid upward, revealing a bit of well-toned thigh.

I told her.

"It was that easy, huh?" She sipped from her drink.

Maurice jumped up on the bed, circled three times, and then laid down facing me.

Nan and I talked for hours. It isn't that I intended to delay the inevitable, it's that I had time. I had time and I could bill it all to Nan's husband.

She told me about Maurice's ribbons and trophies. She told me about all the luxuries Ed gave Maurice, and she told me about all the luxuries Ed could afford but wouldn't share with her. He never beat her, but it was still a marriage made in hell. I once heard that the opposite of love isn't hate, it's indifference. That's the relationship they had.

Perhaps it was just the light, but as we talked I realized how beautiful Nan was. She wore a simple skirt and blouse, no make-up, her long brunette hair pulled back in a simple ponytail. There was no bitterness in her voice and every so often her eyes sparkled.

By the time Maurice scratched at the door to go out, I had fallen for my client's wife. I had fallen hard and fast and deep, and Nan hadn't done one damn thing to encourage me.

I stood in the doorway, watching Nan and Maurice as the dog sniffed around the tires of my car, finally watering one. With the sun setting behind her, Nan's figure was clearly silhouetted under her thin cotton clothes. My body responded to the sight even though I tried to think of other things.

When they returned to the room, I didn't step away from the door. I turned sideways to let them pass. Maurice brushed against my legs. Nan's hip brushed against my upper thigh, the swell of one breast brushed against my arm.

Inside the room again, the door closed and locked behind us, Nan asked, "What now? Do you take me back?"

I told her it didn't have to be that way. She stood less than a foot away and I gathered her into my arms, pulling her to me until I could feel her heavy breasts flatten against my chest.

She tilted her head back and looked up at me. Her eyes sparkled and I knew it wasn't the light. "So how will it be?"

I covered her mouth with mine and she melted into my arms.

We kicked poor Maurice off the bed twice during the night.

The following morning I phoned Weinberger. When he answered, I told him I'd found his wife.

"Anything else?"

"She's been shacking up with Maurice."

"Is he okay?"

"The dog's fine," I said. "So's your wife."

"How soon can you get back here?"

"Your wife doesn't want to return."

"To hell with her, just bring the dog."

After I hung up the phone, I told Nan she'd been right. Her husband's only interest had Alpo breath.

I had a long talk with Nan about her future. She already knew how to change her appearance, so I taught her how to change her identity. Within a week she had a new birth certificate, new social security number, and a new driver's license.

"So what happened to her?" Angelou asked.

I shrugged. "Disappeared again."

"Just her and Maurice?"

"I heard from them once, a phone call in the middle of the night about two months ago. She said they were happy. Maurice barked," I told Angelou. "I didn't ask where they were and she didn't say."

"So why'd he hit you?"

"I told Weinberger if he treated his women like he treats his dogs, maybe they'd stick around."

"That can't be all."

I shrugged. "And I sent him a bill for three thousand dollars, my fee for finding his wife. He wants his retainer back."

"For that he hit you?"

"Some guys are funny like that," I said.

GAYS AND DOLLS

THEY ALL WANTED a piece of him, the gays and the dolls. All of them. Because he was a pretty boy.

He had the kind of face that got him pussy on the outside and would turn him into pussy on the inside. That's why he was careful. That's why he would never be caught.

But maybe he wasn't careful enough.

The first time Charlene came on to him, Little Stevie turned away and ordered another shot of bourbon. He'd been waiting at the bar for almost an hour but he knew the rules. Never mix business and pleasure. Never.

That's why he ignored her.

She tried again, but this time she leaned close and whispered into his ear. "Look," she said, "you leave with me or you're out of it completely."

He turned slowly and looked at her carefully. Even in the dim light of the bar, he could tell she was a looker. Braless under the white silk blouse, her massive breasts and stiff nipples were evident through the diaphanous material. Raven black hair tumbled in loose curls down to the middle of her back. Her lips, thickly coated with glossy red lipstick, were full and ripe, and her dark blue eyes glared at him.

He lifted the shot glass to his lips, tilted it back and quickly downed the bourbon. He hadn't expected a woman, but he could adapt. That's how he'd gotten as far as he had. That's why he still walked the streets while all of his old friends were on their way inside or waiting until they could come back into the world.

Little Stevie stood, straightened his pants by pulling at his crotch the way ball players sometimes did, then held out one elbow for Charlene. She slid from her stool, slipped one hand through his arm, and the two of them walked out together.

Once on the sidewalk outside, Charlene guided him toward a waiting limousine. The back door opened and Little Stevie slid into the dark recesses. Charlene slid into the front seat, then turned to face him.

Beside Little Stevie sat a thick block of muscle with closely cropped hair already graying at the temples. Vinnie "The Butcher" Barducci closed one hand over Little Stevie's. Simply closing his hand into a fist would crush Little Stevie's hand beyond repair. They both knew it, so when Barducci spoke, Little Stevie listened.

Little Stevie was a home invader, a slender guy who could get in and out of any house and any business short of Fort Knox without leaving a trace of himself behind. He worked alone, knew his fences better than they knew themselves, and had never been convicted. He had only once been arraigned but the case had been dismissed when the evidence against him disappeared before the appointed trial date.

Barducci explained what he wanted and Little Stevie's already pale face grew whiter still. When Barducci finished, Little Stevie said, "Ameche? You want me to steal something from Don Carlos Ameche?"

Barducci nodded.

The color slowly returned to Little Stevie's face.

THEY LET LITTLE Stevie out of the car nearly ten blocks from his apartment. He walked home slowly, ignoring the cacophony of the street — car horns blaring, jazz drifting through open doorways, sounds of people talking, laughing, yelling. His apartment was a third-floor walk-up in a part of town best known for its night life, a part of town where he could enter and exit his own apartment any hour of the day or night without rousing suspicion. It was the perfect place to live for a man with his chosen occupation.

And it was his chosen occupation that had gotten him into this situation. Vinnie "The Butcher" Barducci wanted him to steal something from Don Carlos Ameche. Don Carlos Ameche certainly wouldn't want to be stolen from.

Little Stevie felt as near to death as he'd ever felt before. If he failed to perform the job, Barducci would kill him as an example to others. Barducci certainly hadn't gotten his nickname carving beef and poultry.

If he performed the job, and Ameche ever discovered he was involved, Ameche would have him killed as an example to others.

He made his way up the staircase to his apartment. As he keyed the lock on his apartment door, his neighbor poked her head into the hallway. She was a statuesque blonde with wide hips and pendulous breasts that he'd once thought he'd like to get into the sack.

Until he discovered that only Holland had bigger dykes.

"In a bit early tonight, eh?" Marcy asked.

"Yeah," Little Stevie told her. "I don't feel well."

"Why's that?"

"I've got a bad case of sour stomach."

"I can make chicken soup."

Little Stevie shook his head. "I don't think that'll help me any."

"Suit yourself," Marcy said. "But if you change your mind, I'm sleeping single in a double bed tonight and wouldn't mind fixing a little something for you and your friend."

Little Stevie pushed his door open, told Marcy good night, and then stepped inside. As he pushed the door closed behind him, Little Stevie listened to people partying in the street outside as the sound drifted up to his apartment. He looked around carefully before switching on the light, then crossed the living room, stripping off his jacket as he walked.

"Are you going to do it?" Charlene asked as he stepped into his bedroom, startling Little Stevie and causing him to drop his jacket. She sat in his bed, resting her back against the headboard. She held a shot glass full of bourbon in one hand, an open bottle in the other.

"What the hell are you doing in here?" He didn't bother asking how she got in. After all, he made a living entering places that other people didn't want him to enter, and he knew full well that he wasn't the only one with those special skills.

"That come-on in the bar wasn't just for show," Charlene said. She sipped from the shot glass.

"Business and pleasure don't mix," Little Stevie said. He picked up his jacket and slung it over the back of a chair.

"Our business is finished," Charlene said as she hoisted the bottle. "Drink?"

"Sure," Little Stevie said, resigned to having his life controlled by others. "Why not?"

Charlene retrieved an empty shot glass from the nightstand, sloshed two fingers of bourbon into it, then held it out for Little Stevie. He crossed the room and took it from her, downed the bourbon in one gulp, and then held the empty glass in his fist as he paced.

"Come sit beside me," his visitor said as she patted the bed. "I won't bite." A sly smile slowly crossed her face. "Unless you want me to."

Little Stevie stopped pacing and looked at her, really looked at her for the first time since he'd entered his bedroom. She still wore the diaphanous white silk blouse and her raven black hair fell in loose curls around her shoulders. Most of the lipstick had worn off of her full lips, but she moistened them with the tip of her tongue as he watched. "You're serious, aren't you?"

"You're damn right I'm serious," Charlene said. Her dark blue eyes seemed to draw him in and he stared deeply into them until he saw her hand moving toward her chest.

She unbuttoned her blouse with one hand, starting at the top and working her way down until all of the buttons were unfastened. As she'd opened each button, she'd revealed a thin stripe of skin from her breasts to her belly, but her breasts were still covered.

Charlene smiled. Then she said, "You can stand and watch, or you can join me over here."

She patted the bed beside her, again.

A moment later, Little Stevie joined her. As he reached into her blouse, Charlene murmured into his ear, "Your hands are warm."

Then she didn't speak again because Little Stevie's mouth covered hers. Their lips met, then their tongues. The kiss was hard and wet and deep, and it nearly took their breath away.

The shot glass Charlene had been holding slipped from her fingers and dropped to the floor, spilling the last of the bourbon on his carpet.

Then she wrapped her arms around him and they rolled across the bed in a passionate embrace.

Afterward, they rearranged themselves and she lay with her head against his chest, his arm wrapped around her shoulders.

"There's a way out of this mess," Charlene said. "Without getting killed."

He stared at the ceiling. "Which is what?"

After she explained it to him, Little Stevie smiled.

THE NEXT MORNING, Little Stevie woke up alone. Charlene had gone. The bourbon bottle had been returned to the cabinet. Both shot glasses had been washed and were resting upside down on the drain board next to the kitchen sink.

He showered, shaved, dressed in his best and waited for his call to be returned before leaving the apartment.

"I wouldn't mind waking up next to her myself," Marcy said when she caught him in the hall on his way out of the building.

"I don't think her pendulum swings that way," Little Stevie told her.

Marcy winked. "You never know," she said. "I can be quite persuasive."

Little Stevie only hoped he could be as persuasive as Marcy claimed to be because he'd made an appointment with Don Carlos Ameche.

Less than an hour later, he stood before Ameche.

"Sit," said the old man. He waved his hand at Little Stevie. "Sit. Be comfortable."

A chair appeared behind him and Little Stevie sat.

"So what's so important you need to see me this morning?" Ameche asked. "What could you possibly have to talk about that couldn't wait until tonight, tomorrow, the next day?"

Little Stevie told him.

"You think you can get in and out of my house without getting caught?"

"I already have," Little Stevie said.

Ameche's face fell when Little Stevie reached into his pocket and withdrew a prescription bottle. It had been on the nightstand next to Ameche's bed less than twelve hours earlier.

"You've certainly got balls," Ameche said.

"And I'd like to keep them."

"So tell me this plan of yours again."

Less than an hour later, Little Stevie walked out of Don Carlos Ameche's house with everything Vinnie "The Butcher" Barducci had requested. By mid-afternoon he was sitting in Barducci's limousine with Barducci and Charlene.

"Just like that?" Barducci asked.

"Slick as snot," Little Stevie said, "and no one's the wiser."

"You're a gutsy little guy," Barducci said. He opened the inch-thick folder and examined the contents one sheet of paper at a time. After he'd looked over nearly a dozen pages, he asked, "You've got the code, too?"

Little Stevie handed Barducci a pocket-sized black notebook.

"Every pay-off from every contractor who worked on the stadium," Barducci said. "And I didn't have a piece of any of it."

"You can now," Charlene told him. "Convince each of the contractors that you'll go public with the knowledge if they don't play your way."

Barducci smiled. "It'll be a cash cow."

"You'd think this stuff would be on a computer somewhere," Little Stevie said.

Barducci looked at him. "Don Carlos is an old-fashioned guy. Everything he does is either in his head or on paper."

Little Stevie shrugged. He'd done his part. Now he just had to get out of the way and let the chips fall where they may. He said, "You done with me?"

Barducci had his driver stop the limousine and Little Stevie climbed out. After the limousine pulled back into traffic, Little Stevie hailed a cab and had it take him back to his apartment.

After he'd been home for nearly an hour, he answered a knock on his apartment door to find Marcy standing in the hallway between their apartments. She held a bottle of wine and three wine glasses in her hands, so he stepped aside and let her in.

Marcy opened the wine and filled each of the glasses.

"We expecting someone?" Little Stevie asked.

"Any minute," Marcy told him.

Another knock on the door and Little Stevie answered it to find Charlene waiting.

"You two know each other?" Little Stevie glanced from Charlene to Marcy and back again.

"Who do you think let me into your apartment?" Charlene asked. "How do you think I even knew about you in the first place?"

"So you're —"

"Flexible," Charlene said with a sly smile.

"Her pendulum swings both ways," Marcy said.

Little Stevie shook his head.

"So what are we toasting?" Marcy asked.

"The ball's in play," Charlene said. She looked at Little Stevie and asked, "Did everything go the way it was supposed to?"

"Perfectly," he said.

Then Charlene explained everything to Marcy. "Barducci wants the old man out of the picture. He figured the inside line on the stadium pay-offs would give him two things. Not only would he receive blackmail money from the contractors, but word would get out that Ameche wasn't to be trusted. He couldn't control his own people anymore."

Little Stevie jumped in. "Ameche thinks Barducci is a loose cannon, one that could go off at any time. He needs Barducci out of the picture. Each one has been angling for a way to move in on the other one, but until now neither one has been particularly successful."

"And Barducci didn't get the information he thought he was getting," Charlene said. "If he has time to figure out the code, he'll realize that what he received is a record of his own drug transactions for the past two years — a record the FBI is very interested in."

Charlene glanced at her watch. "In fact, he should be having them as house guests any minute now."

Little Stevie finished his glass of wine and poured himself a second. Things were moving awfully fast for him and he was having trouble keeping up.

Marcy asked, "So the two of you helped Ameche double-cross Barducci?"

"Exactly," Charlene said.

"So who called in the FBI?"

Charlene shrugged. "Could have been just about anybody."

The three of them polished off the bottle of wine, and then Marcy rummaged through Little Stevie's cabinets until she found a bottle of rum. By the time the ten o'clock news came on, they were feeling quite sociable, but not yet toasted.

The news crew had taped the arrest and they watched as Barducci and three of his men were shoved into the back of a police van.

"I never did ask," Little Stevie asked Charlene after Marcy had returned to her own apartment, "but what's in it for you?"

Charlene smiled. "Revenge. Ten years ago Barducci killed my brother. It was the killing that earned Barducci his nickname. Everybody knew he did it and nobody did anything about it."

"You think this makes you even?"

"Close enough," Charlene said as she snuggled against Little Stevie. "Close enough."

Just then, Little Stevie realized he hadn't been careful enough. He'd been caught by a woman.

He threaded his fingers through Charlene's hair and smiled.

LESSER OF TWO EVILS

WE PEELED HIS face with a paring knife, then spread the thin strips of skin on some dirty butcher paper Nathan found under the sink.

When we finished, Mr. Oglethorpe slumped forward in the kitchen chair, his wrists tightly duct-taped behind him. The pulpy mess of his face remained mostly hidden by his stringy gray-black hair.

"Did you hear about the hockey game at the leper colony?" Nathan asked. "There was a face-off in the corner."

Nathan laughed at his own joke, but I didn't. Neither did Mr. Oglethorpe.

Mr. Oglethorpe never laughed. He never screamed, either. The entire time we peeled the skin off his face, Mr. Oglethorpe just stared at me. His steel-gray eyes never even watered.

Nathan slapped my shoulder. "Come on, man, let's get to it."

We left Mr. Oglethorpe in the kitchen and tore through the rest of the house, pulling photographs from the walls, emptying drawers onto the floor, overturning furniture. I started a pile in the center of the living room — television, VCR, stereo, and anything else we found that we could easily convert to cash.

Nathan bounced around, nervous, not sure what to do until I told him. We were buddies, a team that had looked out for one another ever since second grade when some kid tried to take Nathan's lunch money. I laid the kid out with a steel pipe to the side of the head and Nathan had been my friend ever since.

"I can't believe we done that," Nathan said. "His face, man. We just cut it right off."

I didn't say anything.

"Oh, man, we never done anything like that before," he said. "That was so cool."

He bounced away, then returned with a fistful of CDs, old rhythm and blues and do-wop music.

"I gotta calm down," Nathan said. "I need a blunt, man."

He pulled one from his shirt pocket and a gold-plated Zippo from his pants. I knocked the blunt from Nathan's mouth before he could light it.

"Hey, man, you know what that cost me?"

"Cost you more if we get caught."

Nathan dropped to his knees and felt through the shag rug until he found the unlit blunt. He slipped it back into his pocket.

We finished with the living room and the den and moved to the bedrooms. As Nathan tore through the guest room, I worked my way through Mr. Oglethorpe's bedroom.

I found a prepaid calling card on his dresser, a fistful of women's jewelry in his underwear drawer, and three different driver's licenses with Mr. Oglethorpe's picture but someone else's name. Then I found a snub-nosed .38 in Mr. Oglethorpe's nightstand and I slipped it into my waistband.

Nathan bounced into the room. "We need to hurry."

"Why?" I asked. "Nobody will call the police. Nobody will ever know we were here."

"Look at this."

Nathan dragged me into the other bedroom. He'd dumped the contents of dresser onto the bed and I stared at a heaping pile of women's underthings — all sizes, colors, and styles.

"I don't think they been washed," Nathan said.

I looked at the soiled underthings and thought about the jewelry in Oglethorpe's bedroom. "Doesn't matter."

Nathan stared hard a me for a moment. "You going to kill him when we're done?"

I didn't answer.

Nathan's eyes brightened. "You are, aren't you?"

"Who'll even notice?"

Mr. Oglethorpe kept to himself and hardly anyone knew much about him. He maintained his yard, had flowering plants on the porch each spring, ghosts hanging from the trees each Halloween, and a plastic Santa on his roof each Christmas.

None of the neighbors knew how he earned a living and when asked, he vaguely mentioned "contract work." He left home occasionally, but he had no pets and never asked neighbors to watch his home while he was away.

His next door neighbor once received Mr. Oglethorpe's mail by accident — a government check — and that led to gossip. A few of the neighbors thought Mr. Oglethorpe was retired military or CIA, the others figured him for a former postal worker.

"He's got money, though," more than one of them said. "That new Bronco didn't pay for itself."

"Seen him at the grocery store a few times," said another. "Always pays cash from a roll."

Nathan and I had heard the talk. We'd done a few jobs before, breaking into homes and apartments but never scoring any serious money. All the talk about Mr. Oglethorpe had caught my attention and we'd been inside his house only a few minutes when he returned home. He hadn't been expecting company and we'd overpowered him quickly, duct-taping him to the kitchen chair before peeling the skin off his face and ransacking his house.

After we finished tearing apart the main floor, we moved to the basement, finding a clean and well-lit workshop filled with tools we could easily pawn. Nathan carried them up the stairs to join the stereo, television, and VCR while I continued exploring.

I found a padlocked steel door behind an easily-moved cabinet. When Nathan returned from hauling his seventh load of tools upstairs, he found me staring at the door.

"It leads under the yard," I said. I pointed up. "That's the back wall of the house."

"Yeah, so?" Nathan said. "Let's see what he's got in there."

Nathan found a crowbar and worried at the lock with it. I went upstairs and searched Mr. Oglethorpe's pockets until I found a key ring.

When I returned to the basement, Nathan had made no progress. I stopped him and tried each of the keys in turn until the lock snapped open. I unfastened it, then pulled the door open.

As the door opened, a light inside switched on and we found ourselves staring at a doctor's examination room, complete with a gynecological chair that had handcuffs hanging from each stirrup. Neatly arrayed in a stainless steel tray next to the table were a selection of scalpels, alligator clips and silver clamps, a box of latex gloves, a bottle of chloroform, ammonia poppers, and half-used tube of KY jelly.

A video camera on a tripod focused on the examination table and a television and VCR on a rolling steel cart had been placed against the wall next to it.

Polaroid photos of naked women had been thumbtacked to a corkboard and I crossed the room to examine them.

"Jesus," Nathan said. He followed me inside and gently fingered one of the scalpels. Nathan cut himself and stuck the ball of his thumb in his mouth to suck at the thin trickle of blood.

I stared at the photos and some of the women in the photos stared back at me. Each had been bound with rope or handcuffs and their mouths sealed shut with silver duct tape. Most were nude, their bodies splotched with purple bruises. Others were dressed — barely.

The surgical tray crashed to the floor, sending scalpels and clamps scattering across the floor. I spun around to find Nathan struggling against Mr. Oglethorpe's grip, his legs flailing and kicking. Mr. Oglethorpe held Nathan's head against his chest, one hand covering Nathan's mouth and the other holding the paring knife to Nathan's throat.

I pulled the .38 from my waistband and held it in a two-handed grip aimed at both of them. "Let him go."

Mr. Oglethorpe stared at me without comment while Nathan continued struggling against him.

"VCR," Mr. Oglethorpe said, his eyes darting quickly to the left, then back at me.

I stepped to my right and reached for the VCR. One touch brought it to life and then I switched on the television.

On the television screen we watched as Mr. Oglethorpe restrained a struggling blonde woman not much older than Nathan. Her eyes and mouth had been covered with duct tape, her hair pulled back in a pony tail, her white blouse torn half away to reveal a beige bra, and her pleated blue skirt twisted up to her hips. Mr. Oglethorpe pushed the blonde onto the table and fastened her wrists and ankles with handcuffs. While she struggled, her cut her clothing away with surgical scissors, then tore the duct tape from her face.

The woman screamed, but no sound came from the television.

Mr. Oglethorpe slowly dissected the blonde.

Eventually Nathan stopped struggling and his eyes grew wide as the tape played.

Finally, Mr. Oglethorpe killed the woman, slicing her throat quickly and cleanly.

I watched as she bled to death.

"I'll need help, now," Mr. Oglethorpe said. "I can't face the world like this, can I?"

I still held the gun on the two of them.

"Well?" Mr. Oglethorpe said. "I'll teach you everything."

I squeezed the trigger five times and Nathan slumped to the floor.

Sometimes, you have to choose.

PICK-UP LINES

"HAVE YOU BEEN with many women?"

"Sure."

"How many?"

"A few. Not many. I pretend I'm with you."

"But . . . you've never been with me."

"I know. That's why I pretend."

A crimson stain spread across Ellen's cheeks and she looked away — at the people on the sidewalk outside the café's window, at the cars creeping along the busy street, at the "Going Out of Business" sign on the sporting goods store across the way.

"Why me?" She returned her attention to the young man seated across the table from her. "Why not some swimsuit model or —?"

He interrupted Ellen. "It's always been you."

She wet her lips and touched her hair.

"Ever since the first time I saw you, I knew I wanted to be with you."

"So why didn't you . . . ?"

"Six years ago," he explained, "on the number 3 bus. You gave up your seat so a pregnant woman could sit."

Ellen remembered that day. She'd only ridden the bus because her car wouldn't start. "Why didn't you say something?"

"I couldn't. By the time I crawled over the fat man trapping me against the window, you'd already exited. I got off at the next corner and ran back to your stop, but I was too late. You were gone."

"I worked in the Anderson Building, only a few steps from the bus stop."

"I figured as much," he said. "I looked in every building — the ones where guards didn't stop me — hoping to find you. I missed work that day, even lost my job."

His blue eyes sparkled as he spoke and his attention never wandered from her face. Ellen felt her heart beat faster. She pressed a hand against her chest. "Looking for me?"

He smiled, his lips parting slightly to reveal even white teeth. "Looking only for you."

"And you lost your job?"

He shrugged. "It wasn't a good job. I found a better one a week later, at the deli on Pinehurst and 5th."

"Steinway's?"

"I figured you had to eat lunch somewhere." He smiled, showing his teeth again.

"We'd order in two or three times a month," Ellen said. "Usually from Steinway's. It was only place that offered something for everybody."

"Tuna Melt on Sourdough, light Mayo, hold the pickle."

"How —?"

"Ten months and you never came in," he said. "I volunteered to help with deliveries. I must have delivered your lunch a dozen times before I realized where you worked."

"How did you figure it out?"

"Yours was the only order one Friday. You met me at the front desk and I handed it to you."

"I didn't know."

"Of course not," he said. "Nobody notices the delivery guy."

Ellen wet her lips with the tip of her tongue. "Why didn't you say something?"

"I delivered sandwiches for a living. You were — what? — an Account Executive —"

"Junior Account Exec back then."

"What would you have said?"

"I . . . I don't know."

"You would have laughed in my face."

Ellen looked away, remembering how it had been on the fast track, her star ascending.

He motioned for the waitress, ordered refills for their cappuccinos, then returned his attention to Ellen. "You changed jobs a few weeks later."

"I jumped to another agency, big raise, corner office."

"Account Exec."

Ellen smiled.

"I saw it in the trades. I knew your name by then." He sipped at his cappuccino. "The first thing you did was buy a new car. You traded in the Nova for a Volvo."

She remembered the car.

"Light cream, leather seats. Less than a week after you bought it, someone smashed the passenger-side tail light while you were at work."

"How . . . how do you know?"

He shrugged. "You weren't happy when you saw it that night, were you?"

"Furious," Ellen said.

"All alone in the parking garage with a busted tail light. You must have used a few obscenities."

"I may have invented a few."

He smiled. "Who would have guessed that you could talk like that?"

They were silent while the waitress replaced their cups. When they were alone again, he said, "Poor Buddy."

She stared at him now. "And what about poor Buddy?"

"Such a shame, someone throwing that poisoned steak over the back gate. It's okay, though, he probably didn't suffer," he said. "Did you blame yourself for that? I know you cried for days afterward. How long had you had Buddy?"

"Since high school. He'd just turned twelve."

"He shared your birthday, didn't he?"

Ellen felt her eyes moisten and she looked away. Her English Bulldog had been her only constant companion, greeting her each evening. He had outlasted two serious relationships and three short-lived affairs.

"I guess the real tragedy, though, was your accident."

"My accident?" She returned her attention to the young man across the table.

"Did you even see the truck coming?"

Her hand shook, rattling her cup against the saucer. She lowered them to the table.

"A hit-and-run," he said. "Knocked you into the gutter and didn't even stop to check on you, did he?"

She stared at him now.

"How long did you lay there before help arrived? An hour? Two?"

Her voice was barely a whisper. "Almost two."

"It's a shame Sweeney & Troy wouldn't hold your position open," he said. "Still, six months is a long time to wait for an employee's return."

Ellen said nothing.

"Nice of them to offer you the receptionist's position, though. Keeps a few dollars rolling in."

Ellen pushed back from the table and reached for her brace. She fit it around her arm and grabbed the handle. Then she reached for the other brace.

He reached across the table and placed one hand on her forearm. Chills raced up her arm.

He lowered his voice so only Ellen could hear. "How's it feel to be broke, crippled, and alone?"

Ellen tried to pull away.

"Nobody wants you now," he whispered. "Nobody but me."

The handsome young man released his grip on Ellen's arm and she stumbled away, swinging her braces ahead of her and dragging her crippled legs behind.

Ellen didn't look back. She didn't need to. She knew he was watching. Always watching.

SOFT FOCUS

WHEN CHRIS NORWICH opened the blue, pebble-surfaced suitcase, bundles of twenties fell onto the double bed. He diligently counted them all, assuring himself that the entire $100,000 was present.

A few minutes later, Norwich — known to his parents, his childhood friends, and the KGB as Nikolay Bitov — stood in a phone booth half a block away from his motel room. "I received your gift, Senator," he said into the phone, making no effort to disguise his voice. Beside his elbow, on the phone booth shelf, a cassette player droned out the sounds of heavy construction.

"Where are the negatives?" the Senator demanded.

Norwich smiled, his thin lips barely visible under his walrus moustache. "You should have thought of them before, Senator. The hundred thousand was only for the prints."

On the other end of the line, the Senator gagged. "You —"

Norwich cut him off. "Sorry. A deal's a deal."

"But —"

"I'll call you again someday." Norwich hung up the pay phone, tucked the tape player under his arm, and walked quickly back to his motel room. He knew the hundred thousand was only nuisance money to the Senator, a powerful attorney who'd made his millions before entering politics. More importantly, Norwich knew that as long as he retained possession of the negatives and never became too greedy, the Senator could be nickeled and dimed forever. Norwich remembered the days when he'd had other reasons for contacting Senators, reasons that rarely ever involved money changing hands, reasons that had most often involved votes and committee decisions. Times had changed since then. So had Norwich.

Once back in his motel room, Norwich transferred the money from the Senator's suitcase to his own brown leather case. A few of the twenties found their way into his wallet.

He quietly finished packing his clothes in his other suitcase, then he carried all three cases to the rental car parked just outside his motel room door. He left the key hanging in the room's door handle when he drove away a few minutes later.

Nine blocks away from the motel, Norwich spotted a Goodwill deposit box, pulled the compact Chevrolet over to the curb, and dropped off the Senator's Samsonite. Lacking a gorilla to destroy the luggage, or a train to throw it from, Norwich felt secure dropping it in the Goodwill box. By the time the police found the suitcase — if they ever even looked — enough winos would have pawed over it to have obliterated any stray fingerprints he might have accidentally left on the pebbled surface.

Norwich drove east from the state capital. The morning sun glinted from the highly polished hood of the car and he squinted against it, glad to finally be traveling home. He'd been away almost two weeks, visiting the Senator, two Representatives, and a key cabinet member. He'd planned the trip for almost a year, knowing that he would soon be called home to the mother country, and knowing that he didn't want to leave the United States.

A few minutes past eleven, Norwich peeled the brown moustache from his upper lip, swearing as it pulled at his tender skin. He shredded the false moustache as he drove, throwing the loose hair out the car window. Then he reached into his jacket pocket and retrieved a pair of glasses with thick black frames and clear glass lenses.

Twenty minutes later he entered the next town, a modest-sized city not far from the capital. He drove the Chevrolet into a small rent-a-car lot and parked before the office.

"Was the car satisfactory, Mr. Edwards?" asked the buxom blonde behind the counter when he presented his keys.

"Yes," Norwich said. "Just fine."

She matched the number of his key to a record sheet, then walked out to the car to check the odometer. Norwich admired her wiggle as she walked out and back. When he was younger, he had spent hours between the sheets with congressional secretaries who didn't look half as good as she did.

The blonde returned to her place behind the counter and quickly calculated his bill. Then she looked up and smiled as she gave him the total. "Leave this on your credit card?"

Norwich pulled cash from his wallet, then waited for his change. After receiving it, he picked up the two remaining suitcases and walked south along the main drag to a parking garage where he'd left the other car.

As he left the city limits driving a blue Ford, Norwich pulled off the glasses and watched for the rest stop he knew was coming up. Before long, he stood inside the rest stop men's room staring at his reflection in the scratched mirror above the sink. He carefully removed a pair of false eyelashes and popped the brown-tinted contact lenses from his eyes. He crushed the tiny glass orbs and dumped them into the trashcan. Then he washed his face with cold tap water, removing the thin layer of make-up that had darkened his skin to an olive tone. Satisfied with his appearance, Norwich peeled off his jacket, returned to the car, and continued driving east.

He turned the radio on and listened carefully to the news. Hearing nothing of interest, Norwich searched out a soft-rock station to keep his ears busy. Half an hour later, he pitched the glasses out the open passenger window onto the roadside. In the rearview mirror, he watched them tumble over the embankment and into a weed-choked gully.

As he drove, Norwich smiled to himself. It had all been so easy to do. When the Senator realized that Norwich wasn't kidding about the photos — especially when Norwich had been able to describe a birthmark on the young woman's left buttock — he'd been more than willing to pay. The other three men had been just as satisfied with Norwich's photographic skills and they'd all paid.

This time it had been money. In the past, other Senators and other Representatives had given him the votes he requested. Some of those who refused had had their political careers shortened considerably.

There'd even been one presidential aspirant who'd driven off a bridge with a pregnant woman in his car. In Washington, D.C., nobody knew Norwich's name, but they all learned that he played the game well.

Norwich glanced at the brown leather suitcase on the seat next to him. The money he'd collected from the four men was his insurance against the future. With it, he could disappear into mainstream America before his superiors in the KGB even knew he was defecting.

Within an hour, Norwich had switched cars again, leaving the rented Ford at the airport's rent-a-car lot and retrieving his own car from the airport's long-term parking garage. He transferred the suitcases to his Buick, checked his trunk to see that all of his photographic equipment remained still intact, and began the final leg of the trip home.

By the time he crossed town and pulled into the parking lot behind his studio, Chris Norwich looked nothing like the man who had left behind photos of the Senator performing sexual acts with a woman who not only wasn't his wife, but who wasn't even old enough to vote.

Norwich unloaded his camera equipment. As he carried the last bag into the studio and closed the door, a voice interrupted his train of thought, making his smile disappear.

"What do you need the money for, comrade?"

Norwich stared at the revolver in the other man's hand.

"It was a nice job," said Konstantin Lomeiko, Norwich's contact for the previous eight years. "What you did to the Senator and the others. But the disguises, ah, a bit much, don't you think?"

"You followed me?" Norwich dropped the last suitcase to the floor.

"You've grown old and fat and slow, my friend. Now, tell me, what's the money for?"

Lomeiko stood across the room from Norwich, near the blue screen Norwich used as a backdrop for his studio photos. Between them stood a camera and a heavy-duty flash mounted on a tripod.

"You wouldn't understand," Norwich said. "You haven't been here long enough."

"I've never trusted you, Nikolay. You work too slow, take too much time."

"I've always followed orders," Norwich said.

The gun in Lomeiko's hand never wavered. "And now?"

"And now it doesn't matter what I do," Norwich said. He began pacing back and forth. "I suspect you will kill me regardless."

Lomeiko smiled. "You can be replaced," he said. "You've outgrown your usefulness here and I suspect there is nothing for you to do at home. You will not be missed."

"And the money?"

"Perhaps I will keep it. No one need know about it."

Near the camera now, Norwich's hand snaked out. His thick fingers came down on the flash unit, firing it. Blinded by the sudden flash of light, Lomeiko's hand wavered. He squeezed the trigger. A window exploded in fragments of glass.

Norwich dove at the other man, driving him to the floor. Norwich slammed his fist into Lomeiko's face twice, then he tore the revolver from Lomeiko's grasp.

Breathing hard, Norwich knelt beside the other KGB agent. "Old and fat and slow," he said. Then he pressed the muzzle of the gun against Lomeiko's temple and pulled the trigger. It was his last official act, his .38 caliber letter of resignation.

Moments later, Norwich walked down the street with only a brown leather suitcase in his hand and new identification in his wallet. He hadn't had time to properly pack for his trip, but he knew how to improvise. After all, he had spent years doing just that.

He looked forward to retirement.

FRESH KILL

"THE SON-OF-A-BITCH fired me." Bobby Thornton crashed angrily around the living room. "After eight years, the bastard fired me."

"The kids are asleep," Susan said softly. She'd been asleep herself when she'd heard the pickup slide to a halt in the gravel parking lot outside their mobile home. Now she sat quietly in the living room, holding a frayed blue robe tightly around herself. "Please don't wake them."

Bobby stopped in the center of the room, suddenly aware of the silence around him. He scratched at his belly through his blue flannel workshirt, belched up some of the beer he'd been drinking ever since Martin had given him the news at the end of his three-to-eleven shift, and looked squarely at his wife. "What are we gonna do now?"

They'd bought the mobile home from Bobby's uncle for a few thousand dollars, but it sat on a rented lot. The truck still had a dozen payments to go. The freezer contained a roast, some hamburger, and two dressed rabbits Bobby had shot the last time he'd gone hunting. The cupboards were nearly empty. Susan would have to go grocery shopping with Bobby's last paycheck, and it wouldn't stretch far. It never had.

"We'll get by," Susan told him. "We always have."

"That's all we ever done," Bobby said. "Just get by. How come we don't never get no breaks?"

Susan smiled wanly. She loved Bobby — she'd loved him almost from the moment they'd met — even though she knew he wasn't the smartest man she could have hitched herself to. She didn't answer his question.

"And to think I useta go huntin' with him and everything, just like we was best buddies and all." Bobby finally dropped into the lounge chair, scratching his arm on the frayed edge of the strip of electrical tape holding the imitation leather arm rest together.

"Did Martin tell you why you were fired?"

"He didn't say nothing." Bobby rubbed at the scratch on his arm, his thick fingers massaging the tender spot. "He just said I was fired. I hadda clean out my locker and leave. He didn't fire nobody else."

Susan nodded, took a deep breath, and held it for a moment. She'd known the day was coming. Martin had warned Bobby about his temper. "Did you hit somebody?"

Bobby shook his head.

"Yell at somebody or swear at somebody?"

Bobby shook his head again, the muscles in his deeply-tanned neck still straining with tension.

Susan took another deep breath. Bobby's temper came and went so fast that sometimes it was gone before she even knew what had provoked him. But he'd never hit her and he'd never hurt the children. She couldn't say as much for the bedroom door. They'd replaced it twice during the three years they'd lived in the mobile home.

"I gotta go to the unemployment office tomorrow," Bobby said. He ran one hand through his short brown curls, pushing them back away from his forehead. "I don't like it there. They gonna ask me why I lost my job. I ain't gonna know what to tell them."

"I'll go with you," Susan said. She would have to help Bobby with the forms. Sometimes the questions confused him. The government never made the forms easy to understand. "Maybe Mama will sit the kids."

Bobby grunted. He was glad he had Susan. She made everything all right. She always had. Ever since high school. Since before high school.

"We'd better get to bed," Susan said. "Tomorrow's going to be a long day."

TUESDAY THEY WENT to the unemployment office and filled out forms. Wednesday they went to Public Aid for food stamps. Thursday Susan went to the mill to pick up Bobby's last check.

Martin came out of his office when he saw her. They talked quietly for a few minutes, exchanging pleasantries about the weather. Finally, he asked, "How come you stay with Bobby? He'll never amount to much."

Susan knew what Martin meant. In high school twenty-two years earlier she'd had her choice. She'd known that Martin was going to inherit his father's mill and all the money and responsibility that went with it. Still, she'd chosen Bobby.

Martin hadn't needed Susan but Bobby had and Martin had never understood the difference.

"There's still a chance," Martin said. He'd spent the years alone in his house at the top of the hill, his only company an elderly housekeeper who came in three times a week. "I'm still waiting."

Susan shook her head. She'd been beautiful once, was still beautiful to Bobby and Martin, but the years had taken their toll on her. The creases around her eyes had grown deep and her auburn hair was now flecked with gray. Softly, she said, "You'll die waiting."

Martin shrugged his shoulders, rubbed distractedly at the rounded belly causing his white shirt to pull at the buttons, and said, "If it's not enough, let me know." He motioned vaguely at the check Susan held in her hand.

She stood a little straighter, making herself as tall as Martin and as much more dignified as she could in the homemade print dress she wore. "It'll be fine. I'm sure you've paid Bobby everything you owe him."

Then she turned and left. Susan wouldn't take charity from Martin and was offended that he would even offer.

When she arrived home an hour later, Susan found Bobby on the front porch with his rifles. Junior and Ruthie played on the rusting swing set Susan's sister had given them when her own children had outgrown it.

"Going hunting?"

Bobby put down the rag he'd been using to clean his .22. "Tomorrow. Early. Leave before the kids wake up."

THE NEXT NIGHT he returned home with a squirrel.

"Best I could do," he explained as he placed the carcass on the kitchen counter. He'd dressed the squirrel where he'd shot it, leaving the waste behind for the crows.

"It isn't much," Susan said, disappointed. Bobby had always fed the family from his hunting. Even when jobs were scarce, he always put fresh meat on the table.

"Two shots," Bobby said. He placed the empty .22 shells on the counter next to the squirrel carcass. Susan had taught him early to bring the shells home. She wanted to be sure Bobby wasn't spending more on ammunition than she would have spent on the same amount of meat at the grocery store.

But Bobby's father had taught him well. He was a good shot, and his efforts were rarely wasted.

"THE BANK CALLED today," Susan said. "They wanted to know why we've missed two payments on the truck. I told them you lost your job and we don't have any money."

Bobby had come home empty-handed again. He laid his rifle on the table. The past two months had begun to wear on him.

"They said they'll repossess the truck if we don't pay something soon."

Bobby took the last bottle of beer from the refrigerator, unscrewed the cap, and took a long, slow drink. Then he walked outside to the pickup.

An hour later he had the truck up on concrete blocks and all four tires safely locked in the wooden shed he'd built the first year they'd lived in the mobile home.

When he went back inside, Bobby said, "We're gonna have to walk."

Susan had expected to. In '84 Bobby had put their old Chevy up on blocks the same way. The truck couldn't be repossessed in the middle of the night if it couldn't be driven.

"I sold some food stamps to Margie," Susan said. "And I paid the electricity bill today. The manager says he'll give us a month's lot rent free if you'll help him clear out that stand of trees back behind his place. He wants to store up some firewood for winter."

★　　★　　★

"HOW COME YOU'VE been avoiding me?" Martin asked when he caught up to Susan in the parking lot of the grocery store. He pulled off his red hunting cap and wiped at the sweat on his forehead, using it to plaster his thinning black hair back across the top of his head.

"I haven't been avoiding you," Susan explained as she lifted Junior out of the shopping cart. Ruthie tugged on her jeans. "I just haven't seen you around."

"Look," he said, nervously glancing down at the two kids huddled close to Susan's legs. "I had to fire Bobby. He was screwing things up. I've got a business to run, you know."

Susan nodded. Business had always come first with Martin.

Ruthie tugged on Susan's jeans again. She said, "I haveta pee."

"In a minute," Susan told her daughter.

"Do you need a ride?" Martin asked. "I could take you home."

Susan shook her head. "It's not far."

She lifted two shopping bags out of the cart and began walking toward home, her children following closely behind.

BOBBY PULLED A second shirt over his thick chest. The weather had been growing colder every day and soon it would snow.

He looked into the mirror glued to the closet door. He'd stopped shaving as soon as he'd felt the first nip of October and his beard had thickened. If he planned to be out in the cold, he had to keep his face warm.

After he buttoned the second shirt, Bobby pulled on a heavy jacket his kids had given him the Christmas before when everything had been going fine.

Susan rolled over in bed and looked at him. She said, "Good luck."

"I'm gonna need it," Bobby responded. "I ain't had none in a long time."

Susan's wan little smile returned, spreading itself across her pale face. "We're getting by."

The day before, the sheriff had made Bobby put the tires back on the truck and a man from the bank had driven it away. Bobby's last unemployment check had been cashed, and most of it spent. The power company had sent a warning but Susan had thrown it away before Bobby had a chance to see it.

Bobby kissed his wife gently, then he quietly left the mobile home and began the long walk to the lake. He'd left the .22 at home, instead carrying his deer rifle. In a small backpack, he carried twine and a dozen plastic garbage bags. On his hip he wore a finely sharpened Bowie knife. If he shot a deer he would have to dress it in the field — like he did the rabbits and the squirrels — and carry the best meat home on his back. He'd done it before. His father had taught him how because his mother had thrown up the first time she'd seen an animal dressed. So Bobby brought the meat home to Susan, never showing her where it came from.

"I HEARD YOU'RE not eating so well," Martin said. He'd stopped Susan as she'd come out of the Public Aid office. He'd been on his way to the Post Office just down the block when he'd seen her come around the corner of the building, holding the throat of her jacket closed against the bitter wind.

"We're doing okay."

"I know it's been rough on you," Martin said. "It's been a bad season. I don't think anybody's bagged their limit. I know I've tried."

"Bobby does okay. We eat."

"Why don't you come up to the house for lunch," Martin suggested. "We could talk about old times."

"I'd rather not. I have to watch the children."

"Where are they now?"

"With Mama."

"Let them stay with Mama tomorrow, too," he suggested. "Come up to my place. Stay with me for awhile. I'll take care of you."

"Bobby takes care of me."

"I can do a better job. You know I can."

Susan hesitated.

Seeing Susan's hesitation and not understanding the reason for it. Martin said, "Come see me. Spend time with me. I'll feed your family."

Bobby stepped around the corner, his heavy boots crunching in the ice and snow. He pretended not to have heard anything they had said and he stood next to his wife, glowering down at his former boss and one-time classmate.

Martin nodded at the bigger man, then hurried off down the street without a parting comment.

"What'd he want?" Bobby asked.

Susan answered slowly. "Nothing, Bobby. Nothing I'd ever give him."

THE WORST SNOW storm of the winter hit town the day after the power company shut off their electricity. They spent the night huddled around a pair of kerosene heaters the mobile home park manager loaned them.

The next day Susan sold the last of the food stamps to Margie for only half what they were worth so she could get the electricity turned back on.

The cupboards were empty by the end of the week, except for the box of Cheerios they hadn't dared open yet and the box of rice Mama had sent home with the Chinese-dinner-in-a-can they'd eaten the week before.

Bobby, dressed in multiple layers of clothing, headed down the road toward the lake. If he didn't bag something soon, the family wouldn't eat. And he'd never let that happen. Never.

He arrived at the lake as dawn crept over the horizon, and he'd been there almost three hours before he saw the tracks in the snow.

The tracks were small but distinct and he followed them through the trees, quietly stalking his prey just the way his father had taught him. Within ten minutes he spotted a tiny blur of red in the trees ahead of him and Bobby knew what he'd found.

Anger flared through him — anger that he'd tried to suppress for the past months. He rushed forward, quietly as he could, took aim at the blur of red he'd become so familiar with over the years, and squeezed the trigger.

The sound of his rifle echoed across the lake as Bobby bent to retrieve the spent shell casing. Then he hurried forward, the anger already dissipating, but not the determination to feed his family.

Using his Bowie knife, Bobby quickly reduced the carcass to its most easily transportable form, packed the fresh meat in the plastic garbage bags he carried, and strapped the entire bundle onto his back for the long walk home.

Bobby's family was going to eat fresh meat for dinner that night and Martin was going to keep his promise to Susan. Martin was going to feed the family.

SHARING

JESSIE AND BILLY were deer hunting when they spotted a captivating blonde carelessly and noisily tromping up the wooded path in her blue Nikes, a green backpack improperly balanced on her rounded shoulders, her unrestrained breasts bouncing up and down under a navy-blue T-shirt. The blonde's long, tanned legs extended shapely from a pair of designer jeans cut off ragged just a pinch lower than her crotch.

Billy elbowed his taller companion and pointed through the trees. "You see that?" he asked quietly.

Jessie stared in the direction Billy pointed and nodded silently.

"Where in hell did she come from?" Billy asked. The nearest road threaded through the mountains nearly six miles from where they stood.

Jessie shook his head. "Don't know."

Without noticing the two men, the blonde walked past their hiding place and continued up the gentle slope of the path. She whistled the tune of a popular rock song, but neither of the mountain men recognized it; they rarely listened to the radio and never listened to rock-and-roll.

Cautiously, without either of them expressing the desire, they followed her. They had spent so many years in the woods that stealth came second nature to them, and they stalked her the same way they stalked their dinner.

Jessie and Billy had sealed their friendship in Vietnam when they were the only survivors of a gook night attack on their position in the delta. They'd endured a lot of ribbing from the city boys when they'd first enlisted, but their mountain upbringing had helped them become the only men in their squad to walk away when the fighting became a real life-or-death struggle.

After their discharge in '71, they returned to the Ozark mountains of southern Missouri to live the way their fathers had taught them, as a pair of the few true Ridgerunners left in the Ozarks. They had both been born and raised in the backwoods and, except for their voluntary stint in the Army removing communism from the rice paddies of Southeast Asia, they had spent their entire lives living off the land and swapping deer hides and bear steak to the craftsmen in town for the money to buy what they couldn't make themselves.

"You think she's alone?" Billy whispered to his companion.

"Must be," Jessie replied. He scanned the path back along the way the blonde had come. "I don't see nobody else."

Jessie clicked on his rifle's safety, a bullet already in the chamber, and cradled the gun in his big hands as he followed Billy from tree to tree.

A gentle breeze blew down the long slope of the mountain and caught the blonde's shoulder-length hair in its grasp, flinging fine strands of ash-blonde hair over her backpack. She ran her thin fingers through her hair and tucked it behind her ears.

Jessie and Billy paused when she came to a small clearing. They waited until she had crossed before they continued following her trail.

"She's headed for the lake," Billy said. He had always been the most vocal of the pair, able to keep both ends of a conversation going during some long winters when Jessie had let him do just that.

When they caught up to the blonde, she was whistling another unfamiliar tune between bites of a chocolate bar she'd taken from her backpack. When she finished the last bite of melted chocolate, she licked the tips of her chocolate-stained fingers and dropped the brown and white wrapper on the dirt path.

Jessie picked the wrapper up a moment later and stuffed it into the front pocket of his tight-fitting jeans. He didn't litter on the mountain and he wouldn't allow anyone else to either. Jessie understood the mountain. He'd never understood Vietnam and he'd relied on Billy for everything while they were there. When they returned home, he'd continued to rely on Billy.

Billy slapped a small hand against Jessie's shoulder and whispered, "Damn, look at that ass on her." He looked up at Jessie. "How'd you like to have her, Jessie? Get your big hands on her and give her a good squeezin'?"

Jessie smiled at the shorter man, the grin almost hidden by the thick brown curls of his beard. "She ain't gonna let us."

Billy's tight, thin-lipped grin was wicked, and the glint in his eye was one that Jessie didn't like. It reminded him of the night in 'Nam when they'd stolen the colonel's Jeep for a joyride into a rice paddy. They'd had to leave it stuck in the mud and walk six miles back to camp.

"Just you wait and see, Jessie," Billy assured him. "She's going to beg us for it. I guarantee it."

Jessie smiled, but he didn't understand what was going through his smaller friend's mind.

A half mile further along, the path turned at the lake's edge and followed the shoreline for nearly three miles before it began a steep assent up the mountain and then down the other side. The blonde finally stopped walking after she'd been following the lake's edge for nearly a mile.

A wide grassy patch ran almost to the lake's edge and the lake itself was still and clear. The blonde dropped her backpack onto the grass and kicked her Nikes off. She dipped one toe into the cool water, then waded in up to her ankles. A moment later she walked back to her pack and stripped off her clothes.

Billy whistled softly from his hiding place in the trees as he watched her.

Within moments the blonde was swimming easily with long, overhand strokes that carried her along the water's smooth surface. After half an hour, she swam in close to the shore, then stood in waist-deep water and rinsed her hair.

"It won't be much longer," Billy assured his large friend as they peered through the trees.

Finally the blonde left the water and took a red and white beach towel from her backpack. She spread it across the grass and positioned herself on it to dry. First she lay on her stomach, then rolled over and tucked her hands under her head. Within moments she fell asleep, snoring lightly as the cool breeze off the lake massaged her smooth skin.

"Now's the time," Billy whispered as he nudged Jessie with his elbow. He led Jessie from their hiding place in the trees and quietly moved the blonde's clothes and her backpack far from her reach. Loudly, Billy said, "What are you doing up here, ma'am?"

The blonde awoke with a start and reached for something with which to cover herself. The only thing within reach was the beach towel under her buttocks and she struggled to pull it around her body.

"Ain't no call to be doing that," Billy told her as a grin crossed his face. "My friend and I just thought you might be likin' some company, see'n as how you're so far from home."

"No," she said uneasily. "No, thank you. I'm fine."

"I was just thinking we could be sociable, maybe offer you something you don't have," Billy said. The wave of his arm indicated the backpack and the clothes that they'd removed from within her reach. "And maybe we could get a little something in return."

She held the towel tightly around her torso and scrambled to her feet. She shook her head negatively, her gaze shifting quickly from one man to the other and back again.

Billy's hand lashed out and slapped her face, the force of it sending the blonde to her knees in the grass.

"Now there's no need to be gettin' unfriendly," Billy told her. "We wasn't planning on hurting you none. We just wanted to share the wealth, you understand. You've got something we want, and we've got something you want. Ain't that right?"

Billy motioned with the barrel of his rifle and said, "You just lay that blanket out there and maybe we can get started."

When she didn't move, Billy grabbed the beach towel from her grasp and threw it on the ground beside her.

"Straighten it," he insisted.

She turned her back to him as she carefully adjusted the towel.

Jessie watched as Billy laid his rifle aside and stripped off his plaid shirt and faded jeans. He remembered the time he'd stood watching for M.P.s while Billy had a slant-eyed hooker in Da Nang and left without paying. It had served Billy right when he'd come up with a case of the clap a few days later.

"I want you to beg me for it," Billy instructed.

The blonde shook her head again, the ash-blonde hair swinging wetly behind her. He slapped her face a second time, leaving red welts.

Jessie laid a meaty fist on Billy's bare shoulder. "There's no need to be hurting her, Billy," he said patiently.

The blonde looked up at the big man.

"Shut up," Billy commanded Jessie. He turned back to the blonde. "You hear me? I want you to beg for it, 'cause you're going to get it one way or another."

She cleared her throat, sucking on a few drops of saliva to loosen the dryness.

Billy stepped away and grabbed his hunting rifle. He pulled the bolt back and slammed a cartridge into place. "You better beg now. You ain't going to get a second chance."

The blonde's voice cracked, but she began to beg.

"That's more like it," Billy interrupted her as he returned the rifle to the ground beside Jessie. "Keep begging." He glanced over his shoulder. "See, Jessie, I told you she'd be beggin' for it."

Then Billy pushed the blonde over on her back, half on the beach towel, half on the damp grass. He knelt between her legs.

Billy ran his hands across the blonde's stomach, her abdomen, then up her rib cage to her breasts. His thumbs stroked her stiff nipples. She squirmed under him.

"That's enough of that," Billy said. He pinned her wrists to the ground, then pressed his mouth against hers, forcing his tongue between her teeth.

He released one of her wrists and reached down between them. He forced her thighs apart.

"You're gonna like this," he said. Then he moved up and onto her and into her. He pulled back and pushed forward, straining against her, again, and again, and again, until suddenly he cried out. He lay still for a moment, breathing heavily, and then he rolled off of the blonde.

Jessie stood over them, his rifle still cradled in his thick arms, watching wordlessly, his thoughts returning to Vietnam and all the things he'd done because Billy had insisted.

The blonde found the bile in her throat and spit in Billy's face. Billy wiped it off with the back of his left hand and slapped her again with his right.

The blonde raked her clawed hand across his cheek. Skin and hair peeled off under her sharp nails and Billy reeled backward from the unexpected blow. Blood trickled between his fingers as he reached up to touch the four long, thin wounds.

He screamed at her, his voice echoing faintly across the lake. "You're never leaving this mountain." He scrambled away and turned to Jessie. "Shoot her," he demanded. "She's going to leave here and tell the whole world what you tried to do."

Jessie stood with his rifle in his meaty hands, a silent mountain of a man. His eyelids narrowed to slits as he considered what had happened and what Billy was telling him.

The blonde tried to slowly back away, fear glazing her pale blue eyes.

"Shoot her and get it over with, Jessie," Billy demanded. "We're done with her. Shoot her quick and we'll dump her body in the lake so nobody'll ever find out it was us."

Jessie unsnapped the safety on his rifle, aimed the barrel at the blonde, and considered. A single bullet sat in the chamber, waiting.

Jessie said slowly, the words coming as hard as the thoughts behind them, "I shared a lot with you Billy. And sometimes I done wrong 'cause I shared." He still had nightmares about the time he'd shot a shoeshine boy because Billy had told him the boy was a Viet Cong come to slit his throat. He would wake in a cold sweat, the expression on the boy's face etched in his mind, the sound of Billy's laughter echoing in his ears.

Billy looked at him wildly, not comprehending what his big friend was saying. "Shoot her, damn it," he screamed at Jessie. "You done everything I ever told you to do. What are you waiting for?"

Jessie knew Billy was right. He had followed the weasel-faced Ridgerunner through the rice paddies of 'Nam and he'd come back to the mountain when it was over because of Billy. But he wasn't in 'Nam anymore. He was home now — home on the mountain where he understood how things were supposed to be.

"Damn it, you ape, shoot!"

Jessie swung the rifle a few degrees to the right and pulled the trigger. The butt of the rifle slammed into his shoulder as the hammer snapped down. The bullet entered Billy's hairless chest just above his heart and blew away the back of his rib cage as it came hurling out the other side. Blood and shards of bone splattered the blonde's chest and Billy's dead body jerked with spasms as it fell to the carpet of grass.

Jessie lowered the rifle and looked at the frightened blonde. She shivered despite the heat.

"You better wash up," Jessie told her as he laid the rifle aside. He kicked her clothes and her backpack across the grass toward her. "I'm done sharing with Billy."

TAKING BETS

I SAT AT the bar and nursed a bottle of light beer. Next to me, a broad-shouldered man pushed back the brim of his baseball cap and laughed at the bartender's crude comment about the size of the hooters on the blonde sitting at the end of the bar near the door.

"She's got a pair of Goodyear blimps trapped inside that sweater," the guy in the baseball cap shot back.

"Wonder what the landing gear looks like, eh, Vance?" the bartender said as he popped the cap on a Budweiser and slid it across the bar.

They both laughed, then the bartender lumbered down the bar to serve someone else. Three or four guys reached over the top of those of us occupying the bar stools, trying to flag his attention. The sounds of the Saturday night crowd nearly drowned out the Country music wailing from the juke box.

Suddenly, the blonde yelled and pushed herself off the bar stool. The right shoulder of her sweater and most of her right side had been soaked with beer. She grabbed the elbow of a brunette who'd been standing behind her. "You cunt, look what you did!"

"What I did?" the brunette shot back. "You bumped me." She wrestled her elbow out of the other woman's grip. "You should offer to replace my beer."

The song on the juke box ended and the bar grew quiet. The crowd around the two women backed away and no one moved to restart the music.

"Like hell I'll replace your beer. You owe me a new sweater."

The guy next to me leaned over. "The brunette's spunky, but my money's on the blonde."

Suddenly, the blonde pushed the brunette backwards and stood. The brunette came back at her, grabbing a handful of blonde hair in one fist, and they began flailing away at each other.

"How much?" I asked him.

He pulled a handful of crumpled bills from his pocket, peeled off a five, and slapped it on the bar. I covered it with a five of my own.

A wild, seemingly uncontrolled right hook from the blonde caught the brunette in the face. She stumbled backward, keeping herself upright by grabbing the shoulder of a corpulent cowboy.

The blonde drove her shoulder into the brunette's mid-section and they crashed against the wall next to the juke box. The brunette brought her knee up between them and used her leg to push the blonde away.

"Bitch!"

The blonde grabbed the brunette's arm and the sleeve of her blouse tore away.

The bartender slammed a Louisville slugger against the top of the bar. The sound exploded through the room and the two women stopped.

"That's enough, ladies," he yelled. "Take it somewhere else."

"Ah, Christ," said the guy next to me. "Just when it was getting good, eh?"

We had no choice but to divvy up our money, each retrieving what he'd dropped into the pile.

By then the blonde had pushed her way out of the bar and the brunette had stepped into the ladies room. I finished my beer and went outside, letting the cool, crisp night air wash over me. I'd taken a room at a motel about a mile away from the bar and I walked slowly along the two-lane blacktop highway.

Victoria had just stepped out of the shower when I pushed open the motel room door. Her pale skin was lightly dusted with freckles and it glistened with droplets of water. She'd wrapped her long blonde hair up in a threadbare motel towel and she stood at the bathroom sink tweezing her eyebrows.

"Anything?" she asked when she noticed my reflection in the bathroom mirror.

"The bartender broke it up too soon."

I settled on the motel room bed and switched on the television, flipping channels until I found an old movie I thought we'd like. Victoria joined me on the bed a few minutes later.

Kim returned while the movie credits were scrolling up the television screen. She dropped onto the bed to my left and struggled to pull off her silver-toed boots.

She smelled of beer, cigarettes, and sweat.

"Where'd you get the jacket?" I asked. Her blouse had been destroyed during the fight.

"Guy at the bar."

"That where you been?"

She shrugged. "Just being social."

Kim showered, then joined us in the bed and we watched old movies the rest of the night, not falling asleep until just before the sun rose. We woke at dusk, showered, packed the car, and one-by-one we returned to the bar.

I sat at the bar nursing a light beer while half-listening to the portly guy next to me describe the relative merits of various brands of chainsaws. Victoria sat at a table on the far side of the room, fending off advances from a Gomer with a wedding ring.

Kim waited until Victoria and I had been in the bar for a few hours before she arrived.

"Hey, bitch!" Victoria yelled from across the room when she saw Kim standing at the door.

Kim turned and glared at her as the bar grew quiet.

"Were you in here last night?" the guy with the chainsaw fetish asked. "Those two really went at it."

"I thought I taught you a lesson," Victoria shouted.

"I kicked your whoring ass last night," Kim shouted back.

"Like hell you did!" Victoria screamed as she pushed her chair back and stood.

"I was still here when you crawled out."

The bartender reached under the bar for his baseball bat, ready to slam it against the bar if the two women started throwing punches.

"Wait a minute," I said to the bartender. "If they're so hot to tear into each other, let's let them settle it."

By then Victoria and Kim stood within spitting distance of each other, still hurling insults.

"All right, push back the tables," the bartender shouted. "Make room for the ladies."

Kim grabbed a handful of Victoria's blonde hair with one hand and slapped her with the other. The bartender slammed the Louisville slugger against the top of the bar to get their attention. Two guys in plaid workshirts pulled the women apart.

The bartender said, "If you two are gonna fight, there's gonna be some rules." He stopped and looked at me. "You got any ideas?"

By then most of the tables had been pushed back against the walls, leaving a good-sized circle of cleared floor space. I coughed into my fist, stalling like I was thinking. Then I indicated the open area and said, "You two stay in this area. If one of you gets pushed out, we'll push you back in. No weapons. Fight until somebody quits."

I looked at the bartender and he said, "Okay by me."

The two men holding Victoria and Kim released them. The two women rushed toward one another. Victoria swung first, catching the side of Kim's head with a right hook. Kim moved with the punch and then came in under it and caught Victoria in the abdomen with a solid right.

Victoria doubled over, her heavy tits nearly falling out of her black v-neck sweater.

"Ten bucks says the blonde wins," I said to the chainsaw fetishist.

"You nuts?" he asked. "The brunette's gonna take her for sure."

"Put money on it?" I asked.

"Shit, yeah," he said.

"I want a piece of that," said the guy next to him.

Kim pushed Victoria to the floor and jumped on her. Her tits bounced up and down inside her blouse like twin tether balls.

Victoria threw Kim off and tried to crawl out of the space we'd designated as the ring. A burly guy in a leather jacket stood her upright and pushed her back toward Kim.

Kim grabbed a handful of Victoria's hair and tried to hold her head still while she smacked Victoria with her open hand. I'm sure the slaps sounded worse than they felt, but Victoria struggled anyway. She brought her knee up into Kim's left thigh and pushed her away.

Kim held on tightly and wrestled Victoria to the floor. They kicked and clawed and tore at one another's clothes, and it appeared that Kim had gained the upper hand and was sure to win the fight.

Soon I held nearly a thousand bucks, much of it favoring Kim. Victoria fought her way out from under Kim and pushed herself to her feet, but Kim caught her and pinned Victoria's arms behind her back. By then they both faced me. I reached up and rubbed the side of my nose with two fingers and then Victoria flipped Kim up and over her back.

Kim came right back at her, driving her shoulder into Victoria's stomach and sending both of them into the gut of a burly bearded guy with Harley-Davidson tattoos on his forearms. Even their momentum and their combined weight failed to budge him and he simply pushed them into the center of the makeshift ring.

Kim still had her shoulder planted in Victoria's stomach and her arms wrapped around Victoria's back. Victoria clasped her two hands together into a double fist and pounded on Kim's back until she drove the brunette to her knees. Then she brought her knee up into Kim's face and snapped her upright.

Victoria backhanded Kim across the face, snapping her head to the side. Kim put her arm up and blocked the next blow but it was obvious she had grown weary.

Victoria pushed Kim backward and dove on top of her, straddling the brunette and pinning her arms to the floor with her knees. Then she tore open Kim's blouse, sending buttons flying everywhere and freeing Kim's heavy breasts. Every guy in the place watched as Victoria grabbed Kim's tits, squeezing and twisting them.

"Alright you cunt," Kim muttered under her breath. "I quit. You win!"

Victoria stood and brushed herself off. She looked down at Kim and spit on the floor next to her head. "Don't you ever screw with me again."

Some of the men in the crowd cheered, but most of them grumbled about the outcome. The seemingly humiliated brunette pulled her blouse around her exposed breasts and someone helped her off the floor and into the ladies room.

"That's it everybody," the bartender yelled, still brandishing the bat in case anyone cared to dispute him.

A few minutes later, Kim slipped out the back door.

As I paid off the bettors, Victoria crossed the room toward me. "Buy me a drink?" she asked.

Victoria and I left the bar half an hour later, having made a big deal about going back to my place for a little private wrestling match. Kim waited outside in the car. She'd parked at the darkest edge of the lot, the engine running and the lights out. Victoria and I walked slowly in her direction.

Kim slipped the car in gear as soon as we opened the doors and had the car moving forward before we'd pulled the doors closed. As the front tires bucked up onto the asphalt highway, Kim spun the wheel to the left and we headed north to the next little town where we could pick up a few bucks.

As we drove through the night, I showed my partners the wad of bills I'd stuffed into my pocket after the fight and I said, "We raked in a bundle."

"Next time," Kim insisted, "I get to be the underdog."

BETTER TO HAVE LOVED

THE 747 CARRYING Samantha disappeared into the clouds while I watched from a window inside the terminal. After the plane had been out of sight nearly ten minutes, I turned away and began the long walk back through the terminal to the garage where I'd left my car.

The scent of her perfume still clung to my clothes and the waxy taste of her cherry red lipstick still clung to my lips. If I closed my eyes I saw her there before me, honey-blonde hair framing her oval face, a pair of pale blue eyes staring back at me without remorse. It's been said that parting is such sweet sorrow, but it's much more than that. Parting is the realization that everything you once shared is little more than a slowly fading memory.

As I approached my car, I pressed the electronic device in my pocket, deactivating the auto-alarm. Then I unlocked the door and slid behind the wheel. Instead of bringing the engine to life, I gripped the steering wheel tightly with each hand and leaned my forehead against it, waiting for tears that wouldn't come.

She'd made all her plans without me, had told each of her friends of her decision, had packed her bags and had them waiting in the closet before confronting me with the news of her impending departure.

Samantha had reasons for leaving me, reasons that she spelled out in great detail after she made slow, sweet, delicate love to me for the final time. I tried to convince her to stay, used every argument I could think of, and made every promise that I thought might cause her to change her mind, but nothing did.

At the airport, after learning her flight number, I redoubled my effort, if not for her to stay, then at least for her to take a later flight. I wanted her to remain with me as long as possible, but when the airline announced boarding, she stood, gathered her carry-on luggage in one hand, and stretched up to kiss me for the last time.

I grabbed her, wrapping my thick fingers around her upper arm through the rough wool of her sweater. She glared at me then.

"It's too late," she said as she jerked away. "I'm going home."

I wanted to tell her to stay and I wanted to tell her why, but I couldn't. Instead, I watched her board the plane.

I banged my forehead against the steering wheel one time, wondering if there was any other way I could have prevented her from taking that flight, and realized there was nothing else I could have done without attracting unwanted attention.

Perhaps if I had known Samantha's plans, I could have altered the chain of events set in motion months earlier. But I hadn't.

Two hours after her plane leveled off on its trip across the Atlantic toward Dublin, it would explode. Somewhere across town Sean would phone one of the news services and claim credit on behalf of our organization.

After straightening in my seat, I wiped at my eyes with the tips of my fingers. Then I started my car, slipped it into gear, and backed out of the parking space.

I loved Samantha and would always remember what we had shared, but the organization was my life and would never abandon me the way she had.

BLACK MACK

I RUBBED MY sweating palms on my faded blue jeans and looked out the living room window at my aging red Peterbilt.

"You can't go out there," my old lady pleaded, her voice on the ragged edge of fear. Her blue eyes were red and puffy; she'd been crying most of the evening.

"I'll be okay," I told her.

"But they killed that guy up north a few weeks ago," she said, pushing herself up from the couch and walking toward me.

"I'll be okay," I repeated. "I can't afford to sit out the strike. I've got a $2,800 payment on the truck next week and the company's willing to double my usual fee for hauling a load to Chicago."

Betty fell into my arms, her long brown hair cascading over my thick forearms.

"I don't want anything to happen to you," she said.

"If I don't drive, I lose the truck. You remember what happened during the last strike." We had been two days away from repossession of my truck, hadn't eaten any real food in a week, and I'd damned near taken Fat Freddie's offer for the Harley I had sitting in the garage. I couldn't go through that again.

"I don't care about the truck," she said between tears. "I care about you."

I stroked her hair with my thick fingers and felt her body shake with silent sobs. "The truck, the bike, and you," I said. "That's all I got."

"John," Betty whispered as she turned her face upward toward mine. "Before you go . . . ?"

I took her chin in my hand and held her face while I pressed my mouth against hers. Betty's full red lips parted and I slid my tongue into her mouth, tasting the beer we'd shared during the late news.

Finally I pulled away from her. "It's time to go."

"John?"

"Yes?" I turned from the door and looked back at her. Fear had returned to her face.

"Call me when you get there."

I blew her a kiss, then stepped outside and walked to the Peterbilt. I climbed into the cab, feeling the comfortable bulk of the seat quickly form itself to my shape as I settled into place.

The engine roared to life beneath me and I took one last look at the house, saw Betty standing in the doorway and saw the Harley parked neatly in the center of the garage. Then I drove the truck down the street away from the house and toward the highway. Driving bobtail — without a trailer — made the Peterbilt handle like a two-ton sports car, and I made good time.

Across town, I turned off the highway, downshifted several times, and eased up to a loading dock. I checked with the man in charge, then backed my cab under a load of frozen foods. With help from the guys on the dock — one of them a fellow biker with heavy alimony payments — I quickly hooked up the pneumatic and electrical cables on the truck, double-checked everything myself, then gathered the paperwork and climbed into the cab. I tried my best to ignore the picketers at the far end of the dock entrance. I hated to cross their line, and they hated me for doing it, but this was a question of survival. When I eased the truck toward them, they yelled "Scab!" and worse, but they didn't damage the truck.

My goal was Chicago by dawn and as I eased the Peterbilt and the trailer load of frozen food onto the highway, I realized how easy the trip had been in the days before the truckers' strike, and I realized how many times I'd cruised the same highway with Betty on the back of my bike and the wind whipping through our hair.

I wiped my hands on my jeans, then used the sleeve of my shirt to wipe the steering wheel dry. The highway stretched dark and empty before me and I slowly eased the truck up to the speed limit, and then edged beyond it when I'd passed Smokey's favorite hiding places just outside the city.

Half an hour later my CB crackled and I heard the first of a series of voices shouting "Scab!" as I passed a usually busy truck stop filled with idled semis.

I saw no other trucks on the six-lane highway so I knew the insults were meant for me. Even though I sympathized with my brother truckers, I couldn't afford to let my truck sit idle. For me it was a simple matter of drive it or lose it. I lowered the volume on my CB, realizing that important information might cross the airwaves despite the various insults hurled my way.

The insults from the idled truckers at the truck stop had almost ceased when a new voice crackled through the CB. "Hey there, good buddy in the cab-over-pete," the voice said. "I hope you got your ears on 'cause this here's the strike enforcer. 10-4."

I listened, but I didn't respond.

I pressed my foot a little more heavily on the accelerator, watching the speedometer needle creep past 65 M.P.H. and edge its way toward 70.

"Look, motherfucker in the big red one," the voice called. "We got you in our sights. You won't deliver that load, good buddy."

I swore to myself and snapped off the CB. I couldn't tell if the asshole on the other end was making idle threats or if he somehow meant to keep them. Beads of sweat formed on my forehead. I wiped at them with my shirt sleeve and watched the empty highway stretch into the darkness ahead. The rearview mirrors showed me nothing coming from behind. I was alone on the road.

I relaxed, thinking the strike enforcer was nothing but mouth. After all, Illinois had been a pretty safe state to drive through since the start of the strike.

The further I got from the truck stop, the better I felt. I calmed down, my body slowly becoming one with the Peterbilt I'd driven most of my life. I felt the highway beneath me as the truck continued rolling toward the Windy City.

Before long I was safely away from the city and the truck stops that surrounded it, flying through the night on Peterbilt wings. I watched carefully as I passed an occasional car, or saw one approaching in one of the southbound lanes. I laughed at a candy-ass with an unmodified Honda when I saw him pull off the road cursing and kicking at the bike.

For almost an hour after I switched off the CB, the trip was incident-free. It stayed that way until a brick crashed through the front passenger window as I drove beneath an overpass. I cursed when the glass flew into my bare arms, cutting me with dozens of tiny sharp edges. Cold wind whistled through the broken window and I shivered.

I switched the CB back on, then reached behind the seat for my thick wool jacket. While I put it on and zipped up the front, the CB crackled.

"You deaf, good buddy? When the strike enforcer tells you to pull over, you better pull that cab-over-pete off the fucking road. The next time it'll be worse than a brick." The CB crackled quietly for a moment, then from it came, "You got your ears on, motherfucker?"

I didn't respond. I'd finished almost half the trip and I knew I couldn't stop. I couldn't let the striking truckers beat me out of my truck payment. I couldn't let them destroy everything I'd worked for.

A pair of headlights swept down the on-ramp and gained on me. I glanced down at the speedometer, saw I was pushing 75 M.P.H., and realized the car coming up behind me wasn't any late-night joy rider.

I listened to the insults as the car behind me continued gaining, my anger rising. I grabbed the microphone and shouted into it. "The Windy City Express don't stop his truck for no chicken-assed mothers."

"You'll learn, buddy-boy," came the response.

Before long, a late-model brown station wagon with no license plates cut into the center lane in front of me and the voice crackled through the CB again.

"This is the strike enforcer, good buddy. You pull that Peterbilt off this fucking highway or you're a dead man. You read me?"

The rear window of the wagon opened and a man in a full-face ski mask poked his head out to stare at me. He pointed a gloved finger toward my face, then pulled a rifle from the rear of the station wagon, braced himself carefully, and took aim.

"You had your chance Windy City Express," my CB crackled. "Now you're dead."

I swore. Before I could respond, the man in the ski mask pulled the trigger. A bullet crashed through the remaining glass on the passenger side and struck the roof. I turned the wide steering wheel sharply to get out of the line of fire, but a second bullet punctured the glass in front of me. Then a third bullet ripped into my arm.

I swore again and pulled my foot from the accelerator. The weight of my load helped slow the truck, and the station wagon continued to move on for a moment. Then red brake lights glowed on the wagon's tail and the distance between us closed again.

The CB crackled and I heard a new voice: male and deep-throated.

"This here's the Black Mack," it said, "and I want my good buddy in the cab-over-pete to put the hammer down tight."

I touched my bleeding arm with my good hand — it was sore as hell but I figured I could get by — then gripped the steering wheel with both hands. My left hand felt wobbly, not closing tightly enough around the hard plastic of the wheel. I told myself it was just the wind and the cold.

When I looked up at the road again, the gunman in the ski mask had repositioned himself, aiming at my cab again. I glanced into the left side mirror and saw a black and chrome Mack truck pulling up along my rear in the fast lane. The gunman barked some order to his driver and the station wagon swerved over into the slow lane ahead of me; now the rifleman had a straight-across shot at me through the broken glass of my windshield. He fired, the bullet spitting over my ducked head and blasting out the window beside me as the Black Mack passed me, its chrome gleaming in the moonlight and the red glow of brake lights. The Mack's air horn roared long and hard as its long silver trailer pushed past the nose of my truck and moved into my lane.

I heard a voice swear into the CB, but the broadcast crackled into silence. I pulled off on the gas, leaving the Mack beside the wagon. The man in the ski mask, hanging half out of the rear of the station wagon, twisted to stare at the silver trailer and the night-black cab. He fired at the Mack, aiming for the massive tires, but missed. Then he spun around toward me and fired two more quick rounds. But I had pulled sharply back into the right-hand lane, and his shots disappeared harmlessly into the night..

I stomped on the accelerator, shifted twice, and rammed into the rear of the station wagon, spilling the masked gunman to the highway and under my Peterbilt. If he screamed, the roar of two huge diesel engines drowned him out.

The Mack started to move over into the right lane and into the station wagon, bumping the little vehicle with its big rear tires. The wagon skidded over the gravel shoulder, then corrected itself, shooting back onto the highway and ahead of the Mack.

I heard the scream of the Mack's engine as the driver shifted, pushing the black and chrome rig ahead of the station wagon again. The driver faked a lane-change ahead of the wagon, twisted the wheel again, and let the chrome trailer slam into the side of the station wagon. Ahead of me, the wagon twisted right, then left, then right again, spun out of control onto the shoulder, then nose-dived into an open culvert. The last I saw of it was in my right rearview. It flipped over and landed on its roof. I'd put a good quarter of a mile between me and the wagon when I saw the red and orange flash of an explosion. The sound came a moment later.

The deep voice returned to the CB with a laugh. "Follow me, good buddy," the voice said. "You've got a load to deliver."

I wrapped my left hand weakly around the CB mike. "Black Mack, you suppose we ought do something about those friends of ours back there?"

The CB spit static and Black Mack answered, "Those bastards weren't friends of any trucker, good buddy. You just lay your hammer down as hard as you can now, 'cause you got a load on a reefer gonna get spoilt if you don't. 10-4."

Chilling wind bit my face as it whistled through the broken windshield. As bitter as the night cold was, I felt sleepy. I let my left arm drop to my lap and rest there, feeling thick wetness on the leather seat and on my pants.

"Hey, there, good buddy, you keep awake now," Black Mack called on the CB. "We ain't got but a little ways to go to Chi Town and you owe me 'bout three tall beers."

I laughed, putting my arm back on the wheel, letting my thick fingers wrap around the grip. Black Mack shot ahead on the highway, and I sped up to follow, keeping his yellow and red rear lights right in front of me. Bands of pain tightened across my chest and a fog kept clouding my mind, but I answered Black Mack's call. For the next two and a half hours I followed the black and chrome rig, a two-truck convoy chewing up the highway. The driver's deep voice hammered at me the entire time, joking, singing off-key, talking about roadside women and some damn fine bikes, and forcing me to stay awake when the only thing in the world I wanted to do was sleep.

Just before dawn, almost an hour ahead of schedule, I followed Mack into the truck terminal where I was to deliver my frozen load. Black Mack rolled to a stop near the gate and gave me a long air horn salute as I eased my red Peterbilt to a halt near a loading dock.

Then a wave of nausea swept over me and I blacked out.

When I woke, I was looking up at the Chicago dispatcher. The first thing I thought of was trouble — for me. I shouldn't have passed out in my truck. But I wasn't in my truck. I was in a hospital bed.

"Did you call my wife?" I asked.

He nodded. "She's on her way. She said somethin' about some guys havin' your hog polished and purrin' by the time you get back."

I tried to smile; Betty knew just what I'd be thinking of. The pain in my arm and the painkillers they'd given me made my thoughts and my mouth work slowly, though.

"You know Black Mack?" I managed to ask.

"Sure, Bud McKay. Big guy with a black and chrome Mack. Helluva guy."

"What kinda beer does he drink?"

The dispatcher patted my good arm. "Why don't you just settle back, huh? Think about drinkin' beer later. You almost bought it last night. When we pulled you from the cab of your Peterbilt, you were soaked in blood. Doctor said you was runnin' on empty, just about."

"What . . . what kind of beer?" I repeated weakly.

"Oh, Mack? Any kind. Never mattered, sure as hell doesn't matter now. Helluva trucker but not one for unions. Too bull-head, if you ask me." The dispatcher looked around for nurses, saw none, and pulled a cigarette from his pocket.

"Lousy singing voice, too," I said.

The dispatcher nodded with a grin. "That's the truth. I didn't figure you knew him."

"Yeah," I answered slowly. "He helped me finish the run up here last night. I owe him a beer."

The Chicago dispatcher took a long drag from his cigarette. "Black Mack quit driving years ago," he said. "Would be 65 or 70 by now. His kid was a trucker, too. Down near Bloomington about two weeks ago some goons took potshots at Mack's kid. The kid and his rig went over a guardrail and blew up. Never did find out who did it."

He took another long drag from his cigarette. "The only things Mack had in this world were his kid and his truck. Kept the truck parked in his back yard."

"And Mack? Where's he now?" I asked.

"Downstairs," the dispatcher said. "Everyone was so worried about you . . . McKay was dead before anyone thought to check his rig. One shot punctured his lung, same caliber as the one they pulled outta you. We found McKay slumped over the wheel, clutching a picture of his boy."

The dispatcher and I sat in silence for a long, long time.

ADAM'S RIB

DAY 1

"I TOLD YOU we needed to go into town this afternoon, but *you* were too busy cleaning that rifle of yours. Now look at what it's doing out there."

I stood next to my wife and stared out the window. Snow had been falling heavily for more than an hour, and already it had drifted over the first few porch steps.

"It'll blow over by morning," I said. I took a sip of Scotch from the glass in my hand. "I'll get the Snow-Cat out of the garage and head down to town for whatever we need."

"I told you we shouldn't come up here, didn't I? All we've had since we got here are problems. I told you we shouldn't swap vacation houses with the Carringtons. They're slobs. They don't take care of anything."

"I was sick of Florida," I said. We'd been though it all before. I turned from the window to throw another log on the crackling fire.

"You may be sick of Florida, but the Carringtons are down there, probably taking a late-night swim in our pool."

DAY 2

IT WAS STILL snowing heavily when I stamped my way through the back door into the kitchen.

"The Snow-Cat doesn't start," I said. "Wouldn't you know, the wiring's been chewed right through."

Katrina was standing over the sink peeling potatoes, her long blonde hair pulled into a loose ponytail that hung halfway down her back. "There's some hot soup on the stove," she said without looking up.

I stripped off my parka and my red flannel shirt. The wood-burning stove in the kitchen and the central fireplace kept the cabin well-heated. I could feel sweat begin to roll down my ribcage from my armpits.

I pulled open the liquor cabinet. I needed a shot of scotch, and, if nothing else, the Carringtons kept a hearty supply of booze in the cabin.

"Adam, I had the radio on while you were out," Katrina said as I poured my drink. "They said the snow won't stop for almost 36 more hours. We'll be snowed in for sure."

DAY 4

KATRINA'S ROBE WAS half unzipped, revealing the reasons I'd married a woman 12 years my junior. Her breasts played peek-a-boo through the soft folds of blue cloth as she moved around the bedroom.

"It finally stopped."

I was lying in bed, the quilt pulled up around my armpits, loose threads tangled in the thick mat of black hair on my chest. The cabin was still warm, but the fire had almost gone out during the night. Katrina poked at the cinders, then added a few smaller logs.

"I'll go out and see if I can rustle up a deer," I said. I threw back the covers and swung my feet onto the cold hardwood cabin floor.

"It's about time," she said. "We'll be out of fresh meat in two days if you don't." She padded off to the kitchen while I pulled on my jeans.

THE GENERATOR WAS working fine when I stopped at the garage to check on it. There was enough fuel to keep it running for nearly another month — if we were careful. It was the one thing I'd repaired carefully when we'd first moved into the cabin earlier that fall. Without it we had no electricity. We were too far away from civilization for power lines or telephones. The nearest town was 85 miles down the mountain on rarely traveled roads.

I spent most of the morning in the woods, always in sight of the wisp of smoke that crawled up the sky from the cabin's chimney. I returned with an undersized rabbit for my effort.

As I was dressing the rabbit on the kitchen counter, Katrina said, "Is anybody going to check on us?"

"We aren't due back for more than a month," I told her. "Only the Carringtons know where we are, and they probably don't even know it snowed up here."

"They probably don't even care."

I swore under my breath. She was about to start complaining again. We'd been married four years, and Katrina had spent three-and-a-half of them complaining.

"We shouldn't have come up here," she continued. "I told you that, didn't I? I said we'd have problems, didn't I?"

I whirled around and slapped her with the back of my hand. "God gave you a nose so you could breathe with your mouth shut," I said sternly, my teeth clenched. "Try it for a while."

I'd hit her harder than I'd intended to, and I saw a trickle of blood at the corner of her mouth. She wiped it off with the back of her hand and stared at the drop she'd caught on her knuckle; she was too surprised to respond.

I'd never hit her before, but the blanket of white just outside the door was beginning to wear on my nerves.

"Look," I said as I placed the carving knife on the counter and took her in my arms, "I'm sorry, but there's nothing I can do about the snow. Let's not jump down each other's throats."

DAY 7

I UNTIED KATRINA'S hands, and she rubbed at her wrists where the leather thongs had cut into her skin. She'd been more animated than usual, her thrusting more forceful during our lovemaking.

She was still breathing rapidly, her breasts rising and falling, her nipples still erect. I sat on the edge of the bed and leaned down to kiss her lightly on the forehead.

A second rabbit was waiting on the counter for me to clean; I pushed myself off the bed and went into the kitchen. We were low on most canned goods and relying on what I caught for most of our meals. I glanced down at the slight paunch I had developed since our marriage and realized that a forced diet wouldn't hurt me.

Katrina switched on the radio when she came into the kitchen. "Another severe storm is predicted for late this evening," the announcer said. "Already nearly a dozen deaths have been reported this past week, and officials are predicting that many more will occur before this winter is over. The National Weather Service indicates that this will be the most severe winter on record for the southern part of the state —"

I switched it off.

"So what will we do now?" Katrina whined at me.

I handed her the rabbit. "You cook this. I'm going out to check on the generator before the storm hits."

"I'll bet the Carringtons are at a disco right now —"

"Disco's out," I cut her off.

"Then out dining. I don't know," Katrina said. "But they're sure not huddled around a fireplace."

"I think it's romantic."

"You would," she scoffed.

The cabin shook violently as the wind smacked against it. This storm was worse than the last.

"Yes," I whispered to myself. "I would." I held her tightly. She'd held her tongue these past few days, but I knew how frightened she was. I could see the deep lines in her face, the bags under her eyes.

"You know I didn't want to come up here, Adam. I wanted to go to Florida, didn't I?"

DAY 10

THE REAR DOOR was blocked by snow when we woke, and I couldn't force it. I tried the front door. I fought with it, finally scrapping it open. The snow had drifted up under the porch roof, nearly sealing off the porch from the outside. I used a shovel to dig my way out.

DAY 13

WE WERE COMPLETELY sealed inside the house and hadn't eaten solid food for two days. We still had a dozen cans of vegetable soup and a fully stocked liquor cabinet.

I stood on the front porch and hacked at the wall of white with the shovel. The more I hacked at the snow, the more snow fell on top of me. Behind me, the light from the window flickered and went dead. The generator had run out of fuel.

Katrina yelled for me.

"Light a candle, damn it!" I yelled back at her. "I can't get out."

She came to the door with a candle in her hand. "Why'd they put the garage so far away?"

"It's not that far away," I said. "I don't think they come up here much during the winter."

"I told you they don't take care of things properly. We never should have traded vacation homes with them. I *told* you that, didn't I?"

"Too many times." I had nowhere to turn. I was trapped with her, I was hungry and the lights didn't work.

"What are we going to do?"

"We're going to huddle around the fire and eat soup," I said. "Just like we did yesterday."

DAY 18

"I'M HUNGRY," she said.

It certainly wasn't news to me. She'd been announcing it every half hour for most of the day. The soup was gone. We were still snowed in.

I stood at the sink and sharpened the carving knife. I didn't know when I'd be able to get out again, but I wanted to be ready to clean anything I caught. I had spent the previous day cleaning my rifle.

I took a pull straight from the scotch bottle. The bourbon would undoubtedly be the next to go.

"I'm sick and tired of looking at you," Katrina announced suddenly.

"You stand there so damned calm about all this. We're going to die here, and you spend all your time cleaning your rifle and sweeping the floor and sharpening that knife. What next? You going to redecorate?"

I looked up at her and considered the knife in my hand.

"You bastard," she said. "I don't know why I ever married you. You're a stupid, arrogant asshole. You dragged me up here to starve to death. You knew something like this was going to happen, didn't you? Huh? Answer me, damn it!"

She was hysterical. I poured her a shot of scotch. "Drink this," I said. She knocked the glass out of my hand, and it shattered across the hardwood floor.

DAY 21

EVEN TRAPPED IN the cabin and complaining, Katrina was a sexually stimulating woman. She had smooth white skin, and her summer tan still faintly outlined her breasts and crotch.

But living with her was growing more intolerable each day. When she wasn't screaming at me, she was sleeping. When she wasn't sleeping, she was screaming at me. Her calm moments were becoming fewer and fewer. I wondered how much more I could take.

DAY 27

I HELD THE last bottle of bourbon. I'd just opened it and taken a swallow. My stomach growled loudly. I rubbed my chin through the thick beard I'd grown.

"Is that the last bottle?"

I nodded.

"It figures you'd drink it. Why don't you offer me some?"

I considered her for a moment — she was standing naked before me. If nothing else, the firewood had held up and the cabin was warm. Katrina stood with her hands on her hips, her legs spread apart defiantly, her slender body silhouetted against the fire in the living room.

I set the bottle on the table between us. "Take it," I said. "Take it all."

She grabbed the bottle and took a long pull from it, then another.

"DARLING," she said nearly two hours later. The bourbon bottle was empty and lying on its side near the trash can where she'd thrown it.

When I looked over at her, she leaned back against the kitchen chair and spread her legs invitingly. "Adam, I want you." She rubbed her nipples with the palm of her free hand, bringing them quickly to their full hardness.

I unbuttoned my red flannel shirt and dropped it on the table. She stood and crushed herself against me, running her thin fingers through the thick mat of black hair on my chest. She reached for my belt. I helped her with it. She was drunk and couldn't manage to undo the buckle.

My jeans dropped to the kitchen floor. I stepped out of them and led her into the bedroom.

I pulled one leather thong from the nightstand and wrapped it tightly around her right wrist. I tied the end to the bedpost and then quickly strapped her other wrist and her ankles the same way just as tautly.

She was pulled tightly in four directions — more tightly than she'd ever been before — and she winced once with pain when I pulled the last thong into place. I bent over her taut body and ran my tongue from the soles of her feet to the tips of her fingers. She thrashed back and forth on the quilt while I teased her with my mouth.

Then I pushed myself off the bed and stood over her. I whispered above the crackle of the fire, "I'll be back in a moment."

"What are you doing?" she asked drunkenly.

I quickly returned from the kitchen, then dropped across the bed on top of her. With one forceful thrust I rammed into her. She twisted and heaved under me, straining against the leather thongs. She moaned in my ear. I wrapped my arms under and around her back, and I slammed into her again and again.

"You're going to love this if it's the last thing you do," I told her.

Our sex was hard and fast and Katrina screamed when she came. She screamed again when I raised the knife.

DAY 28

THE RUMP ROAST was just as tender the second day when I reheated it on the wood-burning stove. I was still hungry — so I offered myself another slice of wife.

SILVER LAKE

BOB AND JOE hadn't seen each other in many years when they met at the Oyster Bar. They exchanged pleasantries, each asking after the other's wife and kids. Then Bob said, "They're draining Silver Lake."

Joe choked on his coffee. "They'll find the car."

"With Sally inside."

Joe mopped his face with a napkin, then used another to wipe spilled coffee from the table top.

Bob waited.

Joe lowered his voice and leaned forward. "There's no statute of limitations, is there?"

Bob shook his head.

A buxom blonde in a low-cut white blouse and short black skirt approached their table. Her teeth sparkled when she smiled. "Are you gentlemen ready to order?"

Bob ordered a filet mignon, medium rare, and a dozen oysters.

She turned to Joe. "And for you?"

He blanched. "Nothing," he said. "Coffee's fine. No, I need a drink. Chivas. Rocks."

"Yes, sir," said the blonde. "I'll have that right out."

As she turned and stepped away from the table, Bob's gaze followed the sway of her hips.

Joe leaned forward, drawing Bob's attention from the blonde, and whispered, "How can you eat?"

Bob shrugged. "A man has to do what a man has to do."

Joe's drink arrived. He downed it and ordered another. When they were alone again, he asked, "What are we going to do?"

"I'm going to eat my dinner," said Bob, "then I'll throw a little charm on the waitress and see if she'll help me work off the oysters."

"You haven't changed, have you?"

Bob smiled. "How's that?"

"You're the same arrogant asshole you were in college."

Bob shrugged.

The waitress arrived with his meal.

"The plate's warm," she said as she bent over the table and provided Bob with a clear view into her ample cleavage. She remained bent over a moment longer than necessary, then straightened and turned to Joe. "Refill that again?"

"Keep them coming," Bob offered. "I'll pick up his tab."

Bob ate. Joe drank.

Bob ate dessert. Joe drank more.

The waitress brought the check and Bob laid a trio of bills on top of it. The waitress reached out to collect Bob's money and he placed one hand on hers, lightly pinning it to the table.

"What time do you get off?" Bob asked.

She winked at him. "Depends how good you are."

"I'm staying over at the Hilton," Bob said, "if you care to find out." He told her his room number.

"Eleven-thirty," she said. "Will you wait up?"

"I'm already up," Bob said. He released his hold on her hand. "Standing at attention."

When the waitress walked away, Joe leaned over. He slurred his words when he spoke. "You're really going through with it, aren't you?"

"What?"

"The waitress. You tell me Silver Lake's being drained and we're only days away from spending the rest of our lives in a state penitentiary and you're looking for a place to stick your dick."

"Better to find a place outside the pen than inside," Bob said. He slid out of the booth and helped Joe to his feet.

"Let me call you a cab," Bob offered. "You're in no condition to drive."

"Neither was she," Joe said. "Not that night. Not after what we did to her."

"What we did?" Bob whispered sharply. "*We* didn't do anything.

You screwed up and *I* helped cover it up." He tapped one finger against Joe's chest. "Don't you ever forget it."

The two men glared at each other until Joe lost his balance and leaned against the wall. Bob had the valet phone for a cab and waited with Joe until the cab arrived a few minutes later.

THE WAITRESS ARRIVED promptly at eleven-thirty, knocked lightly, and then stepped inside the hotel room when Bob opened the door. She pressed herself against him, her heavy breasts flattening against his chest.

"You don't waste time," Bob said. Then he covered her mouth with his, smothering her response. Her lips parted and Bob buried his tongue in the blonde's mouth. She sucked it hard.

When their kiss finally ended, the waitress kicked the door shut, then stepped out of her black pumps. Bob picked her up and carried her to the bed, where they reacquainted themselves with one another's bodies.

Afterward, in the dark, her head on Bob's chest and his arm around her shoulder, the waitress asked, "Do you think he suspects?"

"He didn't recognize you at the restaurant," Bob said. "I think we're good to go."

"LOOK," Bob explained, "I know a guy says he can get to the car before the water level drops that far. He'll pull out the body, get rid of the evidence."

"How can he do that?" Joe didn't look up when he spoke. Instead he stared at the headline on the *Silver Lake Gazette*. The headline, story, and accompanying photo confirmed what Bob had told him the night before: the Army Corps of Engineers planned to drain Silver Lake so they could repair a major flaw in the dam.

"Doesn't matter," Bob said. They sat in his car, parked two blocks away from Joe's home. "But it'll cost money, more than I can get my hands on. I need to know if you're in or not."

"Of course I'm in," Joe insisted. "I'm not going to jail for something we did twenty years ago."

"Not *we*," Bob said. "*You.*"

"What'll it cost?"

"A quarter mil."

Joe choked. "I can't —"

"You'll have to," Bob said. "You don't have a choice."

"But —"

"You can get it, can't you?"

"Of course I can get it," Joe said. "It won't be easy, but I can get it." He folded the newspaper in half. Finally he looked at his former college roommate. "Can this guy you know guarantee that the problem will disappear forever?"

"It'll be like she never existed."

"WELL?" she asked when Bob returned to the hotel room.

"Hook, line, and sinker," he said. He crossed the room to where she sat on the bed, wearing only a black underwire bra and black thong panties. "He'll have the money Friday."

She stood and kissed him. Bob reached for her breasts but she pushed his hand away. "We don't have time. I have to go to work."

"Quit," Bob said. "We'll have the money Friday."

"What if something goes wrong?" she asked. "This hotel isn't free."

Bob released his hold on her and she turned away. After she dressed and left the hotel room, Bob stood at the window and stared out at the parking lot.

In three days, they'd have a quarter of a million dollars. In less than a month, Silver Lake would be completely drained. Among the usual debris at the bottom of the lake would be a 1969 Mustang coupe he and Joe had reported stolen all those years ago — empty because Sally had not been inside the Mustang when Bob had pushed it down the hill into the lake.

It had been a set-up from the start — a prank one frat brother played on another. Bob had set up his virgin roommate with a girl from his home town, then he'd gotten Joe drunk before the big moment. Joe passed out halfway through his deflowering and when he awoke, Bob convinced Joe that he'd killed the girl.

"I rolled her up in your cover and stuffed her in the trunk of your car," Bob explained.

Joe sat on the edge of his bed, his face in his hands. "Oh God oh God oh God. What are we going to do?"

"We have to dispose of the body."

"We can't," Joe said. "We have to tell someone."

"Not me," Bob said. An hour later, he'd convinced Joe to follow him to Silver Lake. He drove Joe's Mustang. Joe drove his Corvette. When they reached the Lake, Bob stopped the Mustang at the top of a long, steep hill.

"You want anything?"

"My books," Joe said. "My tapes."

Bob cleaned out Joe's car and carried everything back to his Corvette. Then he shifted the Mustang into neutral, released the emergency brake, and gave the Mustang a good shove. It moved slowly at first, gaining speed as it rolled down the hill, finally splashing into the lake. They sat in Bob's Corvette and watched the Mustang slowly sink.

The next day, Bob met Sally at a nearly-deserted coffee shop on the edge of town. He gave her fifty bucks for her performance.

"Hook, line, and sinker," Bob said. "He never even asked to look in the trunk."

Sally took her fifty bucks and returned home.

Joe had reported his Mustang stolen that day and after filing a police report and an insurance claim, neither Bob nor Joe ever spoke of that night again. The next semester, they had different roommates. After college, they went their separate ways.

DURING A BUSINESS trip years later, Bob discovered Sally waitressing at the Oyster Bar. He took her for drinks when her shift ended, intending only to reminisce about old times, and they'd wound up spending the night in his hotel room. A few months later, Sally had shown Bob a photo of Joe in the local paper, reporting his most recent promotion.

"Think he remembers what happened that night?" she asked as they lay in bed after trying to screw each other's brains out.

"How could he forget?" Bob said. "I'll bet he still thinks he killed you."

They laughed about it, screwed a second time, and then didn't discuss it again until Bob saw the newspaper article about Silver Lake and the Army Corps of Engineers' plan to drain it. That night they'd begun making plans.

AT THE END of her shift Thursday night, Sally returned to the hotel room to find Bob asleep in the bed. She stripped off her clothes and slipped in beside him.

The next morning, Bob rolled out of bed early and paced for most of the morning. Sally watched him for the first hour, then she showered, dressed, and left the hotel room. She said she had shopping to do.

At noon, Bob finally showered and dressed. At three minutes past two, he pulled his rental car to a halt in the parking lot of an abandoned discount store near the Interstate. Two minutes later, a 1969 Mustang pulled into the empty spot to his right. Joe slipped out of the second car and slid into the passenger seat of Bob's rental.

"Do you have it?" Bob asked.

"Every cent."

"And?"

"It's in the trunk," Joe said. "In a duffel bag. Do you have any idea how heavy that much cash is?"

Bob shrugged. He had never stopped to think about it.

"Are you sure this guy of yours can do what he says?"

"Trust me," Bob said. "Have I ever lied to you?"

Joe stared hard at his former roommate.

"Well?" Bob asked. When Joe didn't respond, he said, "Let's see it, then."

The two men climbed from Bob's rental and walked to the trunk of the Mustang. Joe opened the trunk, and Bob reached in for the duffel bag. He opened it far enough to see cash. Lots of cash. He slipped his hand deep into the bag and pulled out a handful of greenbacks.

"It's all money," Joe said. "Top to bottom. One quarter mil, just like you said."

As Bob leaned forward to stuff the cash back in the duffel bag, Joe smacked him on the side of the head with a crescent wrench. Bob collapsed half in and half out of the Mustang's trunk.

Joe glanced around, then grabbed Bob's feet and forced his unconscious body into the trunk. He slammed the lid firmly closed, then quickly slipped into the driver's seat, keyed the ignition, and sped from the parking lot to the frontage road, and then up onto the highway.

FOUR HOURS LATER, Joe arrived at Silver Lake. Twenty minutes after that he found the same steep embankment where they had pushed his car into the water twenty years earlier. Joe stopped the car and climbed out. He pounded on the trunk with the flat of his hand and when he didn't hear any response, he opened the trunk. Bob had not regained consciousness during the trip and he lay half on the duffel bag of money.

Joe tugged the money out from under Bob and dropped the bag to his feet.

Sally stepped from the bushes and Joe turned to face her. "Where's the car?"

"About a half mile back," she said. She wore blue jeans, a loose-fitting T-shirt, and hiking boots. "Nobody'll notice it."

"For twenty years I've had nightmares," Joe said. "Twenty years this son-of-a-bitch has held it over my head and I wouldn't have known any different if you hadn't phoned me yesterday."

Sally stepped forward, away from the trees. "You think it was easy for me?" she asked. "I got screwed twenty years ago, just not the same way you did."

Joe snorted. "You were a cheap slut then," he said. "What are you now?"

"Well," Sally said as she pulled a snub-nosed .38 from the small of her back, "I ain't cheap."

Joe stared at the handgun.

From the trunk, Bob groaned.

"Climb in," Sally said, motioning with the gun's barrel.

Joe glanced in the Mustang's trunk. Then he stepped toward Sally.

She squeezed the trigger and a bullet ricocheted off the pavement at Joe's feet. "The next one goes through your chest."

Bob groaned again. Then Joe climbed into the trunk beside his former college roommate.

Sally slowly walked toward the Mustang, watching for any sudden movement from inside the trunk. As soon as she was close enough, she slammed the trunk closed. Then she walked around the car and reached inside. She released the emergency brake and shifted the Mustang into neutral.

She walked to the back of the car and leaned her ass against it until the car started to roll.

From inside the trunk, she heard pounding and yelling, but she ignored it. She returned the revolver to the waistband of her jeans, hefted the duffel bag over her shoulder, and began retracing her steps to her waiting car.

The Mustang slowly gained speed as it rolled down the embankment to the lake. Sally barely heard the car hit the water and soon she couldn't hear anything at all.

Sally smiled when she reached her car. She knew she would be laying on a Caribbean beach long before the Corps of Engineers discovered a pair of 1969 Mustangs at the bottom of Silver Lake, one empty, the other with a pair of surprises in the trunk.

WHEELS WITHIN

THE WELL-BUILT BLONDE at the bar had been crying, and now her makeup looked as if it had been applied by Tammy Faye Baker. The other men in the place steered a wide path, but I straddled the cracked vinyl barstool next to her.

She glanced over at me, then looked away. I'd grown accustomed to social invisibility, since it's an advantage in my chosen profession.

I ordered something with a male name — Jim, or Jack, or Johnny, I can't remember which — then toyed with the shot glass when the bartender slid it across the highly polished wood to me. "Gonna drink that, or play with it till it dies?" the blonde asked a few minutes later. She had a pleasant voice, but her question carried an unpleasant tinge of sarcasm.

I smiled at her reflection in the mirror behind the bar, then turned slightly so I could face her. "Is this how you treat all the men who sit next to you?"

"Only ugly dwarves like you."

I'm neither ugly, nor a dwarf.

"Your life could be worse," I said.

"Not likely."

"You could be abducted by a three-headed alien and give birth to Elvis's love child."

She almost smiled. "Yeah," she said. "Maybe it could."

"Freshen your drink?"

"Sure. Why not?"

I motioned for the bartender and had him refill her glass.

"Nicolas," I said. "My friends call me Nick. You?"

"Amanda."

I raised my shot glass in silent toast, then downed the drink in one quick gulp.

"What now?" she asked.

"Now?"

"Aren't you supposed to come on to me? Ask me my sign or tell me you think you know me from somewhere."

"We've never met," I said. "And you're a Virgo."

Amanda paused with her glass halfway to her lips. "How'd —?"

I shrugged my shoulders. "Lucky guess."

She brought her drink the rest of the way to her lips and took a sip.

"And the fight with your boyfriend —"

She slammed the glass back down on the bar, spilling part of it over the back of her hand. "What do you know about that?"

"Enough," I said. I slipped a worn brown leather folder out of the inner pocket of my jacket and flipped it open just long enough for her to see the badge inside. "You want to talk about it here, or should we go someplace a little more private?"

I didn't wait for her answer. Instead, I slipped off the bar stool and took her elbow in my hand. She snatched up her purse, then stood and straightened her tight black skirt with her free hand. She allowed me to guide her through the bar and out the door to the gravel parking lot.

My car had been nosed into the first space past the handicapped spot; hers waited at the far end of the lot. We took my car back to her place, a drive that took less than ten minutes, most of it spent waiting for red lights to turn green.

"Why here?" she asked as soon as we stepped into her apartment.

"This is as good a place as any," I said. I crossed the living room to her couch, then sat.

Amanda stood at the door, confused. After a moment of silence, she finally tossed her purse on an old wooden sewing machine cabinet to her left and joined me on the couch.

She sat at the far end, one leg tucked up under the other, and half-turned to face me. Her low-cut blouse puckered open and I could see the upper swell of her breasts. "What about my boyfriend?"

Her makeup still bothered me and I didn't want to look at her as long as she reminded me of a bad painting. I pulled a clean handkerchief from the breast pocket of my jacket and handed it to her. After suggesting she wipe off her face, I said, "Your boyfriend dumped you a few hours ago."

She nodded.

"Did he say why?"

"He just said he was done with me. He didn't want to see me anymore. He already had all of his stuff packed when I got home. He might have been gone already if I hadn't left work a few minutes early."

"Gerry took nearly half a million dollars with him," I said.

She stopped wiping her face and stared at me.

"He took it from the vault at McCaren and Phibbs."

"But that's where I —"

"You gave him the combination," I told her. "You're an accessory."

"But I never —" She started to protest, then realization dawned on her. "He asked me all these questions about what I did. I never thought —"

"Not many people do," I told her. "He's a grifter — a confidence man — and a damned good one."

"But I didn't — I mean I — I never intended to —" She didn't know what to say so she finished wiping off her makeup. She really was a beautiful woman under all that glop. Too bad she didn't realize it.

"We can get it back," I said. "If you'll cooperate."

"How?"

A FEW DAYS later, Amanda and I sat on the veranda of an upscale bistro overlooking the bay. I'd spent a lot of time with her, coming to realize that she was the kind of woman I could fall for if I let myself mix business with pleasure.

The unexpected cash shortage at her company had not been reported to the police, nor had any insurance companies been notified. Instead, the money had simply been replaced after some heated discussions in the executive offices, the safe's combination had been altered, and business had continued as usual.

A man of average size and build joined us a few minutes after we arrived, and he took a seat across the table from us.

Amanda whispered harshly at her former boyfriend. "You used me!"

Gerry smiled as I placed a hand on Amanda's arm to restrain her.

"We can play this any way you want," I told him.

"You're going to put the money back," Amanda insisted.

"We have a tail on you," I said. Gerry glanced around nervously. "We've been watching you for the past week."

Gerry slouched in his seat as if resigned to his fate.

"We can work this one of two ways," I explained. "I can take you in now, or —"

I let the words hang in the air between us.

Amanda finished the sentence. "Or you put the money back."

Gerry started to laugh.

"McCaren and Phibbs is a well-respected company. They prefer to avoid publicity." Suspicions were that they laundered drug money.

Gerry suddenly leaned forward. "Just walk in and hand them the money? Are you nuts?"

"You put it back the same way you took it out." McCaren and Phibbs had not changed any office routines during the few days since the money had disappeared for fear that their clients would learn of the missing funds. As they had for three generations, company officials kept a proper face as each of the senior partners sought to distance himself from the situation.

"I don't have the combination."

"You will."

"Do I have a choice?"

I shook my head.

After the three of us finished lunch and I explained exactly what I expected Gerry to do the following day, we drove from the bistro to the motel where Gerry had rented a room after leaving Amanda's apartment. Gerry showed her the money, all neatly banded and carefully placed inside an otherwise empty computer terminal.

"Computer repairmen are in and out all the time. Nobody thinks twice about it," Gerry explained. "That's what she told me."

"We'll take the money with us," I said as I transferred the bundles of cash into my suitcase. When I finished, Gerry snapped the computer terminal closed and I said, "We'll see you at 11:30 tomorrow."

I took Amanda back to her apartment, but when we arrived, I didn't want to leave. I was keyed up and knew I wouldn't sleep.

She invited me inside and offered me a drink, then when I had the drink in my hand, she disappeared into her bedroom. I dropped onto the couch and waited. When she returned, she wore only a red lace nightie.

Amanda sat beside me and pressed herself against me. She whispered in my ear, "I'm nervous about tomorrow."

"There's nothing to worry about," I told her. My voice caught. I knew better than to mix business and pleasure, but right then it didn't seem to matter. I placed my half-empty glass on the end table, then turned to face her.

She took my hand in hers and placed it on one of her heavy breasts.

"Feel my heart beating," she said. "I'm scared and I'm excited all at the same time."

My own heart thumped like crazy. I reached out and cupped her other breast in my free hand.

AT 11:37 the next morning, Gerry walked into McCaren and Phibbs with an empty computer terminal under his arm and I sat in a rented car outside. Twenty-six minutes later, Gerry returned and this time the computer terminal had been stuffed with bundles of currency taken from the safe.

"How'd it go?" I asked as he slid into the back seat of the car.

"They weren't expecting a thing," he said. "The new guard is just as stupid as the old one. With everybody in accounting out to lunch, there's nobody watching the safe."

I started the engine, slipped the car into gear, and moved out into traffic.

Gerry started laughing. "Amanda fell for it twice."

I glanced over at my partner. I wanted to smile, but restrained myself. As I drove toward the airport, Gerry shoved the computer terminal in a cardboard box, stuffed Styrofoam peanuts around it, then sealed the box shut. At the airport, he would check the box and his luggage through to Detroit.

I had the money from the first heist waiting for me back at my place. It wasn't a perfect split, but we figured a few thousand one way or the other wasn't worth the hassle of counting it all out and dividing it equally.

I dropped Gerry off at the airport, waved good-bye, and then let my smile crack wide across my face as I pulled away from the curb.

THAT EVENING I sat in Amanda's apartment awaiting her arrival from work.

As soon as she came through the door and saw me, she ran across the room and threw herself into my arms.

"Did I do a good job?"

"Perfect." She'd switched the money in the vault earlier in the day. Gerry had left town with thick packets of blank paper sandwiched between real currency. He couldn't have gotten away with enough for a decent vacation and I knew he'd be pissed as soon as he realized it.

"Did I get myself off the hook? Am I no longer an accessory?" The half million dollars Gerry thought he had in his computer terminal now sat in the trunk of Amanda's car.

"Not exactly," I said. "You won't be able to return to work at McCaren and Phibbs. They'll never trust you again."

"But I got their money back."

I would never have said that.

"So where do we go from here?" I asked. Originally, I had intended to stiff Gerry out of his share. I'd never intended to fall for Amanda, but I had and I wanted her with me.

"Don't you have to turn all this money in?" she asked. "File some kind of police report?"

"I never said I was a cop."

Her brow furrowed in thought. "But I saw —"

I reached into my inner jacket pocket and retrieved the worn brown leather folder with the badge inside. I slid it across the table to her.

She examined the badge closely, then said, "Jesus, you really aren't a cop."

"Virgin Islands? St. Croix?"

She smiled.

TOO MANY

MARLENE REACHED OVER the worn wood of the bar, grabbed Kim's long blonde hair, and pulled her half-off her bar stool. Until that moment, nobody in Maxie's had paid any attention to us. Now, even the two bikers who'd been arguing about the outcome of a George Foreman-Mike Tyson match-up turned toward us to watch the two women.

"Look, cunt," Marlene said, her voice as hard as tempered steel, "if I ever catch you around here again, I'll take you out myself."

Kim grabbed the brunette bartender's wrist, sinking her long red fingernails into the tender skin of Marlene's inner wrist and forcing her to loosen her grip. My date pulled her head back just in time to avoid Marlene's roundhouse left.

"You haven't got what it takes, bitch," Kim said. Then she cocked her right fist and buried it in Marlene's face.

Marlene stumbled backward, rattling the liquor bottles lining the wall behind the bar as she crashed into them. She charged the bar, coming half over it before Kim caught her with another right. Marlene collapsed on the floor behind the bar. When she didn't get up, Kim dumped our pitcher of beer on Marlene's head and the beaten bartender came up sputtering.

"Don't ever try that again," Kim commanded. Then she turned and stalked out of the bar.

I watched the door close behind Kim, then I watched Marlene wipe her face with the dirty towel she usually kept tucked in the front of her jeans. I'd known Marlene for two years and when I was sure she was okay, I pulled a crumpled ten from my pocket, dropped it on the bar, and followed Kim out the door. We'd come in together; the least we could do is leave together.

"What the hell was that all about?" I asked when I caught up to her in the parking lot.

"You wouldn't understand."

"Wouldn't understand?" After twelve years as a uniformed patrol officer and three more as a private detective, I doubted if there was anything left that would surprise me. Later, I would be proven wrong.

I slid into the driver's seat and Kim slid in beside me. In the dim light inside the car, she looked none the worse for wear, though her carefully coifed hair was now wildly deranged. I started the car, then drove over the curb onto the street. The springs in my old Ford were so bad it no longer mattered how I treated the car.

"You pack a pretty good punch," I said as I turned left on Evergreen. I'd shared a bed with Kim often enough the previous two months that I knew she liked it rough, but I'd never seen her fight before.

She reached over and slid one hand from my knee up into my crotch. "You liked watching that, didn't you?" she whispered hoarsely in my ear.

I was so hot I ran two red lights on the way to my apartment. Once we were inside my place, Kim pushed me toward the bedroom and stripped off her clothes.

I AWOKE THE next morning when I felt Kim climb from the bed. I pushed myself up and leaned against the headboard, a pillow stuffed behind my shoulder blades, and locked my fingers behind my head, watching her.

"Why'd you take me to Maxie's last night?" I called.

Kim poked her head out of the bathroom. "Marlene's the other woman."

"You could have told me," I said. "I'd have suggested a different bar."

She didn't respond so I swung my legs over the side of the bed, preparing to stand. Kim had first walked into my office three months earlier, settled into the chair on the far side of my desk, and crossed one long leg over the other. Then she leaned forward, providing me with a glimpse of her ample cleavage. After a short discussion during which she mentioned my former partner, she hired me to determine who murdered her ex-fiancé — a fiancé, it turned out, who had been engaged to two women who had not met until his funeral.

My investigation had quickly ground to a halt. The local police — including Lieutenant Eddie Carlson, a man who'd once been my partner in a patrol car — had refused to cooperate, word on the street was non-existent, and I was left with only the knowledge that Antonio Martelli had taken a single .32 slug in the base of his skull. It appeared to be a professional hit, but I could find nothing in his background to tie him to the local Mafioso and I'd told her so. At the time, she'd seemed quite pleased with the results of my investigation, but my increasing physical involvement with her clouded my perception.

I finally pushed myself off the bed and padded to the bathroom where Kim had already climbed into the shower. Over the sound of the shower, she said, "I want to go back."

"To the bar?"

"I have some unfinished business."

I'd done most of my drinking at Maxie's for almost two years and Marlene had served me more often than the other bartender. Despite her seemingly diminutive size, I'd seen her take out a 230-pound biker with a few well-placed punches. "You really don't want to provoke her."

"I don't know what Tony saw in her." Kim silenced the shower and reached out for a towel. "He told me I was everything he ever wanted in a woman. He lied to me."

"He lied to Marlene, too."

"You taking sides?"

The one man who had already divided his loyalties between them had died. I shook my head.

THAT AFTERNOON, I sat in Eddie Carlson's office at the precinct house and asked about Antonio Martelli.

"I thought you dropped that case already." He fired up one of the cigars that had always threatened to drive me from the patrol car to avoid the smell.

"I did," I explained, "but I've been seeing my client socially."

"Pretty hot number, ain't she," Carlson said around the cigar he'd clamped between his teeth. He shuffled a few folders on his desk, then opened one. After he quickly scanned the single sheet inside the folder, he said, "There's nothing new."

"Would you tell me if there was?"

Carlson shrugged. "Friend or not, I still have orders to follow."

I knew about orders. Failure to follow a direct order had led to my early retirement from the force.

Carlson blew out a thick stream of foul-smelling cigar smoke, then said, "Sorry I can't be of more help on this one, Jack, but that's the way it is."

As I stood and crossed his office to the door, he gave me one last piece of advice. "You don't know what you've gotten yourself into."

FOR THE REST of the afternoon, I worked a few leads on another case, trying to track down a former savings and loan vice president who'd swindled her employer out of a few hundred thousand dollars. Night had already smothered the city by the time I called it a day. I phoned Kim's apartment but received no answer, then phoned my office to recover the day's messages from my answering machine. Only my insurance agent had phoned.

On the way to my apartment, I pulled into Maxie's parking lot. It had been a long, hard day and I needed a beer — or two — before returning home.

I was sitting at the far end of the bar — halfway through my second bottle and just about to tell Marlene the punchline of a joke involving two blondes, a midget, and a double-headed dildo — when Kim stormed into the place. All eyes followed her as she marched down the length of the bar, her ample breasts bouncing under her sweater.

Marlene swore under her breath. "What do you want?"

"We have things to finish."

"There's nothing left to discuss."

"He was mine, bitch."

Marlene laughed and brushed her short black hair out of her eyes. "If you'd been enough for him, he wouldn't have come looking for me."

Kim's anger flared and she tried to grab Marlene over the bar, managing to grab the front of her blouse. Marlene quickly backed away. Her blouse tore open.

"You got lucky last time," Marlene said. "You won't be so lucky this time."

She grabbed Kim's hair and back-handed her. Kim tried to step away, but couldn't. She grabbed Marlene's wrist and jerked her forward. They wrestled across the top of the bar until Kim put a lockhold on Marlene's arm and pulled her over the top, sending bottles and glasses crashing to the floor.

Marlene pulled free as she tumbled to the floor, rolled and came up on her feet. She crouched low and ran straight at Kim, catching her around the waist and knocking her down. Kim scuttled away, then slipped in a pool of spilled beer. Marlene dived on top of her and they rolled over and over. As they rolled, the last shreds of Marlene's blouse tore free and she was nude from the waist up.

One of the bikers at the pool table whistled appreciatively. The other said, "Five bucks on the blonde."

As the two women struggled to their feet, Marlene grabbed hold of Kim's sweater. Kim bent forward and backed quickly away, the sweater sliding up over her head and off. Her thin bra was nearly translucent.

Before Marlene could untangle herself from Kim's sweater, Kim stepped forward and landed a roundhouse left to the side of Marlene's head, knocking her over the side of the pool table. Kim grabbed Marlene's hair and pulled her up, spinning her into a full-nelson. Marlene let her knees collapse, trying to drop free, but Kim was too strong and she held her up.

Then Marlene locked her knees, twisted, then suddenly bent forward. Off-balance, Kim flew up and over Marlene's back, landing in a heap on the floor.

As Marlene moved in to take advantage of the situation, Kim grabbed Marlene's ankle and sent her sprawling on the floor. Then they tangled again, their arms and legs entwining in a ball of fury as they rolled across the bar room floor, kicking and biting and screaming. From where I sat it was impossible to tell who was getting the better of the other.

Then suddenly, Kim stood. Marlene lay in a heap on the floor, her breath coming in deep ragged gasps. She'd taken all she could, but she hadn't conceded.

Kim looked down at Marlene.

"I know why he liked you," she said. "You're a tough bitch."

Marlene didn't respond.

Kim took a half-dozen deep breaths before continuing. "But what's mine is mine. I decide when I'm done with it and I'll get rid of it when I am."

One of the bikers tossed Kim's sweater at her and she caught it with one hand. She glared at me for a moment before turning to leave.

I watched her leave, then turned and loaned Marlene my shirt. I sat in my sweat-stained undershirt as I finished my beer.

KIM DISAPPEARED THAT night without saying good-bye and it wasn't until three months later that I learned her true identity. The evening Lieutenant Carlson showed me Kim's jacket — obtained on the sly and unofficially revealed to me — I sat in Maxie's nursing a beer. Marlene stood on the other side of the bar, wiping her hands on the dirty towel she usually kept tucked in the front of her jeans.

"You have lousy taste in women," she said.

I'd bedded a professional killer, a woman whose name had been changed by a federal witness protection program after her testimony against a Chicago mobster, a woman who'd been cuckolded and who had eliminated the embarrassment in the only way she'd ever known. Carlson doubted if they could prove she eliminated her own fiancé and my own investigation had only confirmed that no one would talk about it.

"You put up a good fight," I said.

Marlene winked. "I get off at midnight . . . and again within the hour if you're any good."

I took a long, slow sip of my beer, then I smiled back at her.

IDLE HANDS

THIRTY-SEVEN YEARS LATER, that night still haunts me. Mother and I had returned home from the picture show, me tightly gripping a half-empty popcorn box, my fingers slick and salty, my mother fumbling with the apartment key, spilling the contents of her purse when it slipped from her grasp to land on the concrete stoop. She pushed the door open, then bent to gather her belongings.

"Hurry, hurry," she said. She placed one hand on the small of my back and pushed me into the apartment. "It's time for good little cowboys to be in bed."

I stopped in the doorway, pressing backward against the pressure of Mother's hand. The stench of burnt tobacco and spilled bourbon finally reached Mother and she looked up at my father.

He grabbed my wrist, dragging me into the apartment despite my resistance.

"Leave him alone!" Mother shouted and my father threw me to the floor. My knees barked against the hardwood and the popcorn box tumbled across the room, greasy white puffs spilling like fat snow flakes.

"It's not him I come for." He pulled Mother into the apartment and kicked the door closed.

"Earl —" she started.

He backhanded Mother, snapping her head to the side, a dark curl falling across her face as her hair slipped free of the abalone comb I'd given her that Christmas. Mother touched her lip and I saw blood on her fingertips when she pulled them away.

"You wasn't hard to find," my father said. He grabbed Mother's throat, nearly lifting her from the floor.

I ran at him, crashing against his thick leg and kicking his ankle with the pointy toes of my cowboy boots. He dropped Mother on the couch, then turned and slapped me with his open hand. Twenty years spent laboring in the steel mills of Ohio had toughened him and the blow knocked me into the wall.

He returned his attention to Mother.

"Your sister wasn't none too hard to convince. When I's done with her, she wanted to tell me where you was."

He pulled Mother from the couch. Before she could throw her hands up to defend herself, he hit her square in the face, knocking her backward. The blow broke Mother's nose, but not for the first time.

I slipped away, down the hall and into Mother's bedroom, finding the revolver my aunt had given Mother the night we left Ohio. While my father worked a second shift, Mother and I each carried an overstuffed suitcase from the house to the curb where my aunt and uncle waited in their Chevy Bel Aire. We rode in silence to the train station and, while my uncle purchased two tickets to California, my aunt gave my mother the gun.

I cocked the hammer with my thumb, just as I'd seen done in the movie that night, and carried the revolver two-handed into the living room.

"Leave her alone!" I shouted, but my father didn't stop. One work-hardened hand gripped Mother's upper arm while he pounded on her with his fist. She resisted but she didn't cry. She never cried.

Again, I shouted at him. He still didn't respond.

I closed my eyes and squeezed the trigger, the revolver slipping in my greasy grip, the hammer snapping into place with a deafening roar, and I fell backward, crushing popcorn as I hit the floor. When I opened my eyes, Mother had gone limp in my father's grasp, a single bloody hole in the side of her neck.

My father dropped Mother to the floor and stared at me. "You stupid little shit."

He crossed the room and wrapped one massive paw around mine, crushing nearly every bone in my right hand. Then he took the gun away, dropped it to the floor, and dragged me from the apartment to his old coupe parked in the alley behind the apartment building.

I cried all the way to the state line, finally stopping when we pulled into a motor court a mile inside of Nevada. My father had two quarts of cheap bourbon in the glove compartment and he carried them into the cabin with us.

He sat on the bed, drinking and smoking and glaring at me. "What I do with you, now, Tex?"

I cradled my broken hand in my lap and said nothing, waiting, as Mother had often waited, for my father to drink himself into oblivion. When he finally passed out two-thirds of the way through the first bottle, I emptied the rest of the bourbon onto my father's face and chest and dropped one of his still-lit Camels onto the alcohol-soaked bedsheets.

The bourbon had splashed onto my left hand and it burst into flame just as an inferno erupted around my father. I ran to the door, barely pulling it open with my blazing hand, and ran screaming across the motor court's parking lot until stopped by a young woman who smothered the flames with the skirt of her wedding dress. She held me and we watched the cabin burn to the ground.

My father never escaped the flames and the young woman in the wedding dress and the young man she'd married that afternoon raised me as their own, taking me to the picture show once each month but never, ever offering popcorn.

Thirty-seven years later, as the pain in my hands wakes me time and again, that night still haunts me.

DEAD PRESIDENTS
IN MUDVILLE

BETTY BOUNCED ACROSS the living room, proving there was joy in Mudville. She held an acceptance letter from the nearest junior college and, when she wrapped her arms around my neck, she crushed the letter against the back of my head.

She planted her lips on mine in a kiss of joy and, when she finally bounced away, I discretely wiped away the remains of her Strawberry lipstick.

Betty had earned her GED a year earlier, working days as a motel maid and taking night classes three times a week. Her acceptance into junior college over in Waco finally proved her father wrong. She might just make something of herself after all.

I took Betty to dinner that night at a low-budget Italian place which served heaping quantities of meatless pasta for down-to-your-last-dollar prices, split a six-pack of Lone Star with her later as we sat on the couch in her mobile home and watched a late movie on the local network affiliate, and then around midnight I finally gave her a rib-crushing hug, wished her the best of luck, and drove myself home.

I never saw Betty again.

HALF THE TOWN had seen us together at dinner so the sheriff asked me about it the next afternoon. I told him about the letter, the dinner, the beer and the late show.

"Anybody see you leave her place? See you drive home? Anybody at all can place you someplace other than Mudville last night?"

I shook my head after each question. "Not till 8:30 or so this morning. That's when I left for work. Mr. Grandy's out walking that Doberman pup of his, waved to me as I was getting in my car."

Sheriff Hicks wrote "Grandy" on his notepad, chewed on his toothpick for a moment, then asked, "Know anybody'd want to see harm come to Ms. Cherry?"

"Hell, sheriff, you knew Betty about as well as I did. You know any-body would do her harm?"

That's when he showed me the pictures.

I saw the body on the bed, blonde hair and bits of skull splattered across the bedroom wall, bloody sheets twisted around her lifeless body, but I never saw Betty again. Not really.

I turned away from the photos, took a moment to regain my com-posure, then slipped my notepad from my hip pocket and began asking the sheriff nearly as many questions as he asked me. At that point, neither of us knew much.

Betty had lived in Rivercrest, a mobile home park on the west side of the river, built on a low spot that flooded nearly every spring. Locals called it Mudville.

Her neighbors were an assortment of unemployed or barely employed knuckle-draggers, under-educated single mothers, and older couples scraping by on food stamps and Social Security checks. None claimed to have noticed anything unusual that night after I'd left Mudville. Mid-morning, one of her neighbors, an unemployed single mother, had dis-covered Betty's body.

As editor of the town's weekly newspaper, I later spoke to everyone the sheriff had questioned, learning nothing he didn't already know.

The morning before Betty's body had been discovered had begun just like all the others, far as we could tell. The neighbor kids were horsing around at the bus stop when Betty drove past on her way to the motel. She arrived at work just after eight A.M., punched her time card at the clock next to the front counter and stopped to talk with Sherie Cook. She spent her day cleaning the six occupied rooms after the guests checked out, gave the two unused rooms a light dusting, and then washed and folded all the dirty bed linens, interrupting work around noon to eat her sack lunch in the office with Sherie after using her key to open the soda machine to retrieve two cold Diet Dr Peppers.

She finished her work day by vacuuming the motel office. From the motel, she drove over to McAlister's Grocery where she purchased milk, breakfast cereal, and two apples. She arrived home shortly after five P.M., stopping at the row of mailboxes along the road to retrieve her mail.

She phoned me a few minutes later, told me she had good news to share, and invited me to visit her that evening.

"Why call you?" the sheriff asked, but I suspect he knew the answer.

I serve two nights a week as a PiL — a Partner in Literacy — working with local residents by teaching reading at the town library, and Betty had come to me for help when she'd first decided to work on her GED. She could learn just about anything you took time to explain, but book-learning had proven especially difficult for her because she'd been promoted from grade to grade without ever mastering reading skills.

Then she'd dropped out of high school at fifteen, pregnant by a third-string defensive tackle who only played three minutes his entire senior year, married him upon the insistence of both his parents and hers, and then lost the baby to an inoperable heart defect two days after its birth. Betty's husband returned to his family, but her family wouldn't take her back.

She'd scraped by after that, finally able to stop living on the charity of others and renting a place of her own in Mudville, a single-wide she furnished with garage sale furniture and finally felt comfortable calling her own after ten years in residence.

I had arrived in Mudville at a quarter to six that night and by six P.M. I had her college acceptance letter crushed against the back of my head.

The sheriff already knew the rest.

DURING THE FOLLOWING two days, the sheriff questioned everyone a second time, Sherie surprised Mr. Weedleman by quitting her job at the motel, and Betty's parents drove over from Valley Mills, identified and claimed Betty's body, and had her cremated without any service for family and friends.

"Coroner's report," the sheriff said, tapping a folder on his desk when I stopped in to talk with him about Betty's case. Her death had been the lead story in the weekly paper and I had come to follow up for the next edition.

He continued. "Single shot killed her, bullet through the roof of Betty's mouth and out the top of her skull. Slug went right through the cheap paneling and through the outside wall. We dug it out of a Mesquite tree in the next yard."

"Roof of her mouth?" I asked.

"The bastard stuck a gun in her mouth and pulled the trigger."

I shuddered.

"Anything else?"

"We're following every available lead."

"And, unofficially?" I asked. The sheriff and I had known each other since third grade, when I was the new kid and he'd stolen my lunch money.

"We don't have squat," he said. "Everybody knew Betty. She didn't have an enemy in the world, far as we can tell, and the worst thing that can be said about her is that she didn't get along with her parents."

"You look at them?"

The sheriff chewed on his toothpick for a moment before answering. "She had a small life insurance policy. Her parents are the beneficiaries. It's barely enough money to put her in the ground."

I ATE LUNCH at my desk that afternoon, stopping between bites to transcribe my notes into the computer. In addition to the follow-up story about Betty, I had stories about the city council meeting, upcoming school events, and the Corps of Engineers' latest efforts to prevent annual flooding.

As I worked on the Corps of Engineers story, I saw Sherie drive past the window in a late-model SUV I'd seen parked at Honest Abe's Used Cars earlier that morning. I phoned Abe Cohen, then finished my sandwich, grabbed my note pad, and told Martha Anne that I'd return later.

I found Weedleman sitting behind the counter at his motel.

"Sure cut down on payroll, losing two in a week," he said. "Sorry to lose Betty the way we did, though. Hard-working girl. Found another girl from over in Mudville to take her place, Cassie Johnson. You know her?"

"Know the name," I said. Cassie had been the one who discovered Betty's body, finding Betty's car still in the drive and her front door swinging open long after Betty had usually left for work.

When I asked about Sherie, Weedleman said, "Not in any hurry to replace her. Saves a good bit of money not having to."

"You pay her well?"

"Well enough," Weedleman said. "Been with us eight years, regular raises and all."

"Well enough she can afford to replace her old Nova?"

Weedleman shrugged. "Not my place to say."

We spoke about other things for a few minutes, then I asked to see the register from the night before Betty died.

He showed me six index cards, then let me duplicate them on his desktop copier.

"Sheriff already has all that," he said as I was leaving.

"Yeah," I said, "but I don't."

I PHONED EACH of the guests who had registered that night, quickly dismissing five of them. The phone number of the sixth guest — Mr. R. B. Hayes — had been disconnected. He'd paid cash for his room and he'd scribbled an unreadable number in the space where he should have listed his car's license plate.

I brought this information to the sheriff's attention.

"Already checked into it," he said. "Could be important, but haven't been able to follow up on it."

"Mind if I try?"

"Seems as if you've already been trying," the sheriff said. "You think you can do better'n us, go on ahead."

I drove to Sherie's one-bedroom clapboard house over on Seventh. In her driveway and already half-filled with boxes and suitcases sat the

SUV I'd seen her driving earlier that day. I leaned on Sherie's bell and waited until she pulled the door open.

"Nice car," I said through the screen.

"What do you want, Jack?" she asked. She wore blue jeans and a loose-fitting blue T-shirt. Her blonde hair had been pulled into a ponytail held in place with a rubber band. From a distance, she could have been Betty's sister.

"Tell me what happened that day."

"I already told you. I told the sheriff. I told everybody."

"Tell me again."

"Betty came to work like usual. She did her job, we ate lunch together, she left when she finished."

I showed her my copy of the registration card for room five. "What did Betty find in room five?"

"She didn't find anything," Sherie said. She looked over my shoulder, not into my eyes.

I pulled the screen open and stepped inside. I'm not a big man, but I'm bigger than Sherie. Sherie stepped backward.

"So what did *you* find?"

Sherie backed away.

"He'll return, you know. Whatever he thought Betty had, he still wants," I said. "That's why you're leaving."

"I'm just going to my brother's."

"He'll find you there. Then he'll do the same thing to you that he did to Betty."

Sherie shuddered and turned away. I grabbed her shoulder and spun her back around. Her eyes had grown red and moist as if she were about to cry.

"I didn't mean for this to happen."

"For what to happen?" I demanded.

"Mr. Hayes checked out at 7:30. At quarter till eight, I walked down to the soda machine for a Diet DP. I had to buy one 'cause Betty had the key and hadn't come in yet. The door to Number Five had been left open, so I poked my nose in. He'd left a briefcase." She took a deep breath and continued. "I took it to the office and stuck it under the counter, figuring Mr. Hayes would come back for it. Betty showed up a few minutes past eight."

The briefcase stayed under the counter all day, curiosity finally overcoming Sherie near the end of her shift. She popped the briefcase open, discovering banded stacks of hundred dollar bills. Before Weedleman arrived to relieve her, Sherie stuck the briefcase in the trunk of her Nova.

"You got any idea what that kind of money would do for me?" she asked.

I called the sheriff from Sherie's phone and waited until he arrived a few minutes later. Sherie showed us the briefcase. When we opened it, one stack of bills had a broken band.

Sherie rode with the sheriff to his office where she would make a statement. I returned to the motel and spoke with Weedleman again.

"Hadn't thought anything about it before," he said, "but that Hayes guy did come back. Said he'd left something in his room. When I checked the lost-and-found box, all I found were some old magazines and a wrist watch. He didn't seem upset, but he did seem determined, asked me who had access to the room."

"Betty?" I asked.

"Sure, I told him it was Betty, said he could come back the next morning and talk to her."

"You tell him anything else?" I stared at the time clock and the two time cards slipped into the rack next to it, an employee's name typed neatly at the top of each card.

Weedleman shook his head. "I didn't tell him anything else and he didn't ask."

That evening, I told Sheriff Hicks what I thought had happened and he later confirmed that a Lincoln Towncar matching the one both Sherie and Weedleman claimed Hayes had been driving had been spotted in Mudville around seven that night, about the time Betty and I were finishing dinner at the Italian restaurant.

I USED MOST of what I'd learned for my follow-up story in the next week's paper. Sherie returned the SUV to Honest Abe's Used Cars and Abe Cohen turned her down-payment over to the sheriff. Sherie quietly left town and, after a heated discussion between the sheriff and myself, the confiscated money was divided two ways. The sheriff's department made a healthy investment in new equipment, including a new patrol car, and the town established a scholarship fund in Betty's name at the junior college over in Waco.

That was pretty much the end of things until the following spring when the Corps of Engineers still hadn't solved the problem and the river overflowed again, sending Mudville residents scrambling to higher ground. The river finally receded a few weeks later, leaving a Lincoln Towncar upended on the riverbank. Inside, still belted into the driver's seat, hung the body of a man, a bullet hole in the side of his head, a 9mm Glock later identified as the weapon used to murder Betty Cherry strapped under his left armpit, and three different sets of identification in his wallet, including one for Rutherford B. Hayes.

Federal officials identified the body as belonging to the kid brother of a made guy who imported illegal drugs through Mexico. They conjectured that Hayes had killed Betty in an effort to recover the lost briefcase and had been killed in turn when he failed to recover the mob's money.

The sheriff disliked untidy resolutions and he conspired with the county coroner to list Hayes' death as a suicide. The Corps of Engineers needed two more years to solve the flooding problems in Mudville.

CITY DESK

THE CLATTER OF typewriter keys came to a slow halt when I entered the room. Eight pairs of eyes watched me make my way to the desk in the rear. I hadn't had the limp when I'd left the office that morning; my face hadn't been bloody and bruised either.

Michael O'Shea, a grizzled veteran who still worked the police beat, was the first to speak. "What in hell happened to you?"

Before I could answer, he reached into the bottom drawer of his desk and pulled out a nearly full bottle of bourbon. O'Shea was Irish, but he wasn't a lush. The bottle was for special occasions. This must have counted as one of them. He quickly filled a paper cup and handed it to me.

I tried to smile when they gathered around my desk. The last time anyone had come into the city room looking that bad had been the night our city editor, Jonny Silverman, had smacked his face into a piece of his wife's Revere Ware.

The smile hurt, so I gave it up. "I asked the wrong question," I finally answered O'Shea. Gently, with the tip of my tongue, I felt the inside of my mouth. I was lucky. I was bleeding from the gums, but none of my teeth were loose.

"You still on the Garrison story?" It was O'Shea again.

"I was."

He studied me carefully, his sagging, expressionless face almost masking the disgust I could see in his eyes. I wasn't sure if he was disgusted with me or with himself. I knew he'd given up the Barket story 20 years earlier — after his house had been fire-bombed and his family threatened.

There's only so far a newspaperman will go in search of a story. Some of us reach our limit sooner than others.

BILLY HORNER, a pimple-faced, broad-shouldered intern from City College, helped me to the men's room. He used a damp paper towel to swab away the worst of the blood.

"This isn't Woodward and Bernstein," I told him. I'd seen too many starry-eyed interns from City College. They all wanted to cover the "big story," collect their Pulitzers and retire famous. After three months interning with us, most of them changed majors or became talking heads on television, covering fluff and bullshit for the illiterates.

"I didn't expect it to be," he said.

I coughed, then spit blood and bourbon into the sink.

Billy wadded up the paper towel and tossed it at the overflowing trash can. It skidded over the top, then fell into the urinal.

"I'll take the Garrison story," he said cautiously.

I stared at his reflection in the mirror. "You wanna be a hero, kid?"

"I want off the society page."

I turned to face him. I carefully touched my cheek and felt the swollen jaw. "I look pretty good," I said. "And this was just a warning."

"I can take care of myself." It was a cocky statement, but it had been a long time since I'd heard an intern have the balls to say it.

I considered him for a moment. "Let your beard grow out," I said. "And talk to me later. I want to be alone now."

"Do I get the story?" This kid didn't know when to quit.

"You don't even know what the story is."

SILVERMAN GAVE ME desk duty after the incident. For weeks, I spent the better part of each day tapping out routine stories and pulling copy from the AP wire.

I was rewriting an obituary, adding local details about a dead movie star, when the phone rang. I answered it, "City desk."

"I haven't seen anything in the paper."

I knew the voice. I'd interviewed Garrison many times as part of my duties in covering the city's Board of Aldermen.

"My editor killed the story," I said. But we both knew the truth — I'd never even written it.

"I'm sorry to hear that," the alderman said. "Will I be running into you again?"

"No, sir," I told him. "I've been taken off that beat." It wasn't exactly a lie. I'd asked for a transfer, but I hadn't gotten my new beat yet.

Garrison said goodbye and hung up. I slowly replaced the receiver in its cradle and finished tapping out the obit. I dropped the yellow second sheets into the box so the copyboy could run them downstairs to the composing room. Unlike most major dailies, we had yet to move into the age of electronic journalism.

O'SHEA AND I were the only reporters in the office when she walked in. O'Shea was too absorbed in our competitor's morning edition to notice.

"Yes, miss?" I called from my desk in the back. "May I help you?"

O'Shea glanced up from his paper as she walked past.

"I'm looking for William Horner," she said.

"Who? . . . Oh, the intern. You a friend of Billy's?"

"I'm his sister," she said. "I was supposed to meet him for lunch."

"There was an explosion at the refinery. Charlie Marotta took him up there to cover his first disaster." I stuck out my hand as I stood. "I'm Dan Fox."

She took my hand in hers and shook it gently. "I've heard a lot about you."

"I trust it was all good."

She laughed politely. "Most of it."

I glanced at my watch, realizing I hadn't eaten in six hours. "Mike," I called across the room, "Watch the phones for me. I'm taking this young lady to lunch."

"JUST WHAT DO you have on Garrison that he wants you off his back?" Billy asked. I was having dinner with Billy and Janet at their house. His beard had filled in rather nicely during the last months of his internship, and he'd continued to pester me about the case. I'm no fool though — I'd continued to discourage him.

That I night I wanted to concentrate on Janet. Listening to her voice and watching her eyes made me realize I wanted to know her better — a lot better. But Billy kept bringing the conversation back to business. I knew he wouldn't let up.

"The usual stuff, mostly kickbacks, payoffs and that kind of thing."

"That can't be all, or he wouldn't have come down on you so hard."

I chewed the tender filet Janet had prepared and swallowed before I answered. "Do you ever read the paper you write for?"

"Is this a trick question?"

"In the past four years, six boys in their early teens have disappeared from the South Side — Garrison's ward and the two wards on either side of it."

"Yeah, so? Stuff like that happens in every city. The police think they're runaways." Billy went back to his food.

When I told them the rest of the story, Janet quickly left the room. I could hear her faintly, vomiting in the bathroom.

Billy's fork dropped to his plate, and he slowly pushed the plate away. He looked pale, but his determination was strong. "Then I want the story for sure."

"It's too rough," I told him. "Let the police handle it."

"They haven't done anything yet, have they?"

"Give them time."

"Garrison's probably got half the force on the take."

"Some, maybe," I said. "O'Shea thinks most of the guys are straightforward. But no cop in this town squeals on another cop."

Billy stroked his curly brown beard thoughtfully. "Can you prove any of this?"

"If I could I would have written the story already." I paused. "I've got my sources — damned good ones too — but no solid facts, no witnesses, no evidence. If I went with what I've got, he could have my ass for libel."

"But those two goons who worked you over —"

"Could I prove they were his? Garrison would just deny it."

Janet returned to the room, still visibly shaken. She'd vomited so violently the blood vessels around her eyes had broken, leaving dozens of tiny red spots. I hadn't promised them a pretty tale.

Billy was wrapped up in his own thoughts.

"Don't be a hero, kid. It ain't worth it," I said. "Your internship is over. Go back to school. Finish your classes. And find yourself a job on a small-town weekly."

TWO WEEKS LATER, Janet appeared in the newsroom again. One look at her and I knew it wasn't another dinner invitation.

"Billy moved out last week," she said. "He didn't take much with him, and he didn't say when he'd be back." She'd been crying. She was still puffy under the eyes. "I tried calling the college, but his instructors haven't seen him either."

I wanted to hold her in my arms and bury her face against my shoulder. I knew how good she'd feel tucked under my chin, and I felt the heat rising inside me at the thought.

The newsroom was no place to comfort her. I pulled my heavy jacket from behind the desk — it had been raining for three days straight, and snow had been predicted all afternoon.

"Why don't we go to my place?" I said. "It's only a few miles from here. I can fix you a drink, and we can talk in private."

"No, I'll be all right. Just drop me off at home, and you can come by after work. Okay?"

AROUND SIX O'CLOCK, Michael O'Shea and I were sitting in two seats on an aisle at the back of the Phillips Auditorium. Garrison was scheduled to speak on unemployment in his ward.

O'Shea nudged me gently with his elbow. I leaned over to catch his whisper. He pointed discreetly at a man standing in the wings. "Isn't that Billy?"

I squinted. My eyes had been deteriorating for years, but I was still resisting glasses. For just a moment Billy stepped onto the light to speak to someone, then he stepped back into the shadows.

"It's him," I confirmed O'Shea's suspicion.

"What's he doing with a scumbag like Garrison?" I hoped it was a rhetorical question, because I wasn't planning on answering.

As soon as Garrison finished his bullshit rhetoric, I headed straight for Janet's place. She gave me a drink; I gave her the news.

"I found your brother," I said. "He's with Garrison."

The color drained from Janet's face as she dropped down to the couch across from me. She pulled her legs up under her thighs and crossed them. Her short robe inched its way up her hips. I tried to look away.

"He's trying to be a hero, isn't he?"

"Either that, or he's just plain stupid," I answered.

"He'll get himself hurt," she said. "He told me what happened to you."

She shifted her position on the couch, perhaps not realizing the free shot she was giving me. I loosened my tie. It was becoming hard to concentrate on Billy's problems with Janet's luscious body so temptingly close.

Suddenly a teapot began to whistle in the kitchen. Janet jumped up and padded across the living room. Over her shoulder she said, "I was going to fix myself a cup of tea. Would you like some?"

I answered affirmatively, then I stood and followed her.

She had taken the kettle off the burner by the time I reached the kitchen, and she was stretching to reach a pair of mugs on the top shelf of the cabinet. The powder-blue robe had ridden up to her waist, and I could see the full extent of her lean, tanned legs.

I came up behind her and reached up for the mugs myself. "I'll get those," I said.

I leaned against her, sure that she could feel me pressing against her buttocks. I snatched the two mugs from just beyond her fingertips and placed them on the counter. With one hand around her waist, I kissed her lightly on the back of the neck.

Janet turned to face me. She slipped her arms around my neck and pulled my face down to hers. Our lips met, and then our tongues began a fiery dance inside each other's mouths.

When the kiss finally ended, she asked, "Why don't you spend the night?"

Only then did she take off her robe.

I SAT AT Janet's kitchen table, scanning the headlines of our competitor's morning edition. During the night, the seventh young boy had disappeared from the South Side. He could have been a runaway, but he seemed to fit the pattern only too well. I had a good idea what had happened to him, but I couldn't prove a thing.

Janet, her hair still damp from our early-morning shower together, stood at the stove frying eggs. I folded the newspaper so she wouldn't see the headlines. "Where's your phone?" I asked.

She pointed a spatula toward the living room. "It's by the couch."

I found it easily enough and dialed the city desk. O'Shea answered.

"Have you seen the morning paper?" I asked.

"Got it in front of me," he replied noncommittally.

"You got any information they don't have?"

"Nothing," he told me. "The kid's disappeared. Gone. Like he vanished from the face of the earth."

I thought a moment. "Nobody at the station house willing to divulge a little extra?"

"The cops aren't talking about this one, Dan. Not to me. Not to anybody."

"Okay," I said, "keep trying. I'll be there in an hour."

THREE MEN WERE stringing wire across the office when I arrived. I dropped my coat across the back of my chair and quickly thumbed through a stack of mail that had been waiting patiently for my arrival — a handful of letters, the usual junk mail, a couple of publicity releases and two bulky packages.

O'Shea stomped in a few minutes after I did. He came straight to my desk. "You see what these bastards are doing?" he demanded.

I looked at the three workers. "Rewiring?"

"They're putting in those VDTs," he said. "The company don't tell us. The union don't tell us. Now all of a sudden we got technology." He pulled off his jacket. "It's bullshit!"

"Did you get anything on the kid?"

"Yeah. Just a minute." He hurried to the coffee machine, drew himself a warm cupful and brought it over. After a few cautious sips, he pulled out a thin notebook from his hip pocket. "Edward Johnson, 13, white, small for his age, good grades, former Boy Scout. An all-around good kid. Nobody had a bad word to say about him."

"Except?" I had to ask; O'Shea would never let it go at that.

"Except nothing. He fits the pattern. The worst thing in his background is his parents' divorce when he was five."

I swore under my breath. Before I could sit down again, I was called away from my desk to interview an overweight rock star who'd come to town on tour. His gold album was nearing platinum status, and my editor wasn't going to miss the opportunity to capture a bigger slice of the teen and post-teen audience. For an exclusive interview, I had to sit through two hours of drugged-out banality.

By the time I turned in the feature, the workmen had quit for the day. I got back to the mail. Most of it was junk as expected. I saved the two bulky packages for last. The first was a new paperback intended for the arts editor. The second contained two rolls of undeveloped black-and-white film. I dug the envelope out of the trash can and studied it carefully. My name was neatly penned on the front, but there was no return address — also no stamps or cancellation marks. The film had made its way to me without assistance from the post office.

I looked at the film again. "O'Shea," I called across the office, "who's in the darkroom?"

"Marotta," he answered. "He's on till midnight."

★　　★　　★

"THESE ARE LOUSY photos," Marotta said as he dumped the proof sheets on my desk. "Who took them?"

"I don't know," I said. And I didn't know until I scanned the photos with the magnifying lens I keep at my desk. Almost every photo featured Alderman Garrison.

I was scanning quickly when something caught my eye. I back-tracked to study more closely the photograph that had grabbed my interest.

I studied the three faces in the picture, then reached across my desk to get the afternoon edition. Edward Johnson's class photo stared out from the front page.

"Is this the same kid?" I stabbed a finger at the proof sheet.

Marotta took it from me and stared through the lens. He looked up at the newspaper photo, then back at the proof sheet. "I'll have a blowup in a few minutes."

O'Shea, Marotta and I stared at the 8" x 10" blowup for a long time. It was a sickening scene, but the photo was well-focused. The faces were readily identifiable.

At midnight, after polishing off O'Shea's special-occasion bottle of bourbon and screwing up enough courage, I dialed Alderman Garrison's home phone number. After three rings he answered with a muffled "hello."

"Just one question," I said. "Where do you put the bodies?"

It had been a fool's bravado that had made me call him, and I realized it as soon as I got home. Four burly men were waiting in the parking lot of my apartment building.

The first bruiser grabbed me by the shoulder as I shut the car door and spun me around to face him. The second threw a ham-sized fist into my gut. I doubled over and retched. O'Shea's bourbon clawed its way up my throat and out of my mouth to fertilize the gravel. I lacked the breath to call for help.

A fist caught the side of my head. Two of the men held me. The other two took turns beating me. My eyes puffed up, and my vision began to blur before I realized one of them was pulling his punches.

Eventually, they dropped me to the ground. One stomped on my left hand. Another shoved a heel right into my kidneys.

Finally it stopped. I felt a hand take my wrist and search for a pulse. After that, someone forced something into my mouth. I held it on the tip of my tongue to prevent myself from swallowing.

"He's dead." It was Billy Horner's voice, and it was coming from right next to my ear. "Swallow it," he whispered carefully just before he stood up. "And pray."

"I TRIED CALLING your place," Janet said as she stood beside the hospital bed. "Then I tried the paper. They said you were here."

Billy had slipped me a powerful painkiller. Shortly after that I'd heard the crunch of tires against gravel as their car left the lot, and I begun crawling to my ground-floor apartment.

"I'll be out of the hospital soon," I told her. I'd lost two teeth and I was finding it hard to talk with my tongue getting lost in the gaps.

"That's not what the doctor says."

That afternoon I sat at my desk holding my head. I'd left the hospital without the doctor's approval. I'm sure the nurse was surprised to find my bed empty and my clothes gone, but I knew I had a story to write.

"Look," Jonny Silverman was saying. "We've got the photo of Garrison and the kid. It's disgusting, but it doesn't prove anything for sure. When was it taken? Before or after the kid was reported missing?"

"I don't know," I mumbled.

"Then you'd damn well better find out."

Silverman was the best editor I'd ever worked for, and he had a good reason for everything he said. But in my condition, I could barely think my way through a tuna sandwich. My left hand had been crushed and was tightly wrapped, my face had been beaten to a bloody pulp and most of my interior organs were on the barely serviceable list.

The workmen were still wiring the office around me as I considered my options. I had the photo and some information from "reliable sources." I also had Billy on the inside. O'Shea answered the phone when it rang, then yelled across the office for me.

It was Garrison. "We caught your boy," he said bluntly. "He won't see the sun set." And he hung up.

"Damn it," I said, pounding my good hand against the desk top.

AN HOUR AFTER two men in a speeding Buick had dumped Billy's body outside the newspaper office, Janet sat by my desk with an old green knapsack on her lap.

"This was Billy's," she said. She'd come straight from the morgue. "Billy called me the night you went to the hospital. He said goodbye and told me where I could find this. He didn't tell me what he'd done to you."

"He was just doing what he had to do." I was tired. I felt like I'd been beaten too hard, too many times.

"He told me to get it and bring it to you. He said you'd know what to do with it." She placed the knapsack on my desk.

With my good hand, I unzipped the nylon bag and reached inside. I pulled out a tiny tape recorder and three tapes. I reached in again and came out with two reporter's notebooks filled with hurried but legible notes.

I scanned the notes quickly, then played the first tape. We finally had Garrison dead to rights. O'Shea and I paraded into Silverman's office with evidence on a series of murders even the DA's office didn't know about.

The next day we published a special morning edition. Despite the objections from our legal department, the photo of Garrison and his thug forcing little Edward Johnson to perform a deviant sexual act with Garrison appeared four-column above the fold on the front page. The byline on the lead story was William Horner's.

O'Shea and I had spent most of the night assembling Billy's notes and tapes into that story, but we all agreed Billy deserved the byline more than anyone else.

I'm sure Garrison would have been convicted of the murders — his accomplices certainly were — but an angry father blew the alderman away with a .45 before the police could arrest him.

As for Billy, he collected his Pulitzer for the story. I was proud of him — he'd been a starry-eyed kid with balls.

There's only so far a newspaperman will go in search of a story. I know. I watched Billy Horner go all the way to the end.

YESTERDAY IN
BLOOD AND BONE

1

WHEN THE CITY'S other major newspaper was finally forced to close its doors during the non-recession of the late 1980s, my employer kept a few of the competitor's reporters out of the unemployment line. I sat with one of them, a grizzled veteran of the copy desk named Benjamin "Bucky" Weaver, a reporter who'd once covered City Hall and the police beat, but who now wrote insipid features about retirees for Wednesday's Seniors Section. We sat on a pair of stools and leaned against the worn wood of the bar at deComposing Room, the drinking establishment across the street from the newspaper office where we worked.

"It ain't like the old days," he said before downing the last half of his bourbon-and-rye, "but then nothing ever is."

Bucky styled himself a philosopher, explaining to me how journalism seeps into your blood and into your bones, and I wasn't about to argue with him — especially since he was picking up the tab.

"Hell, I remember the days when this city had four — count 'em — four major daily newspapers, and guys like you'n me had to scramble to score an exclusive." He motioned to the bartender to refill his glass. I could see the liver spots on the back of his hand as he waved it in the air. "Television's ruined all that. If it ain't the locals, it's CNN and CNBC poking their noses in."

"What can we do about it?" I asked.

"Not a damn thing," Bucky insisted. "Our time has passed."

He drained his glass, slammed it against the top of the bar, and called for a refill.

"Haven't you had enough?" I asked.

"Not till your ugly mug starts looking good," he said. He was one to talk, with a flat nose and a mashed-in face that looked like it had been pounded against one too many brick walls.

"You let me call you a cab when you're ready to leave?"

"I've been called worse." Half a smile crossed his face. I could see the gap between his two front teeth, the one that let him spit tobacco juice with reasonable accuracy.

The bartender refilled Bucky's glass and motioned at my unfinished beer. I shook my head and he moved on down the bar to attend to another customer.

"Yeah," Bucky said, "maybe you'd better call me a cab. I ain't going to be in any shape to drive myself home."

"You drink like this all the time?" I asked.

"Jesus, you an A.A. recruiter?"

I laughed. The odds of me recruiting new members for Alcoholics Anonymous were about as good as my winning the lottery without purchasing a ticket.

"I'm just worried about you, Bucky. I've never seen you so worked up."

"I've got — what? — three years before mandatory retirement, I can write rings around any one of the half-wit J-school students they keep hiring, and I know damn well that I'm nothing but a dinosaur standing at the edge of a tar pit getting ready to take a swim." He took a healthy swallow of his drink. "I'm a dinosaur writing about dinosaurs."

"The average age of the population keeps increasing. Soon there'll be more retired people than working people," I said.

"And knowing that does what for me?"

I shrugged, and then I sipped from my beer.

Bucky took a deep breath and let it out slowly. "I went to see Silverman this afternoon. I told him I wanted back on City Hall."

City Hall's my beat and I cover it well. I asked, "What'd he say?"

"He mentioned ice fishing in hell happening first."

I didn't expect anything less from City Editor Jonny Silverman, but I still felt a bit of relief. It had been a long time since any reporter had made a stab at taking my beat from me.

"Jesus," Bucky said. "You don't have to look so damn happy about it."

"If there was ever a reporter with the balls to take my beat away from me, you'd be the one," I said. It was only a little white lie. In his day, Bucky had been a formidable competitor, occasionally scooping me when he worked for the other paper. Unfortunately for Bucky, the sun had long ago set on his day.

"I've still got connections in City Hall," Bucky said. "There's a few people I can still talk to and information I can get that you snot-nosed punks'll never have access to."

Only somebody as old as Bucky could get away with calling me a snot-nosed punk. I asked, "Like who?"

Before Bucky could answer, the bartender refilled Bucky's glass. I had the feeling I'd be sitting at the bar for a long time, so I had him refresh my beer this time.

"Like Alderman Kelvin," Bucky said. "The old fart won't talk to nobody but me. We're two dinosaurs standing at the edge of the same tar pit."

"He's not likely to be re-elected for another term," I said.

"He's not planning to run again," Bucky said.

"How do you know?"

"I told you, we go way back. Kelvin talks to me, tells me things he won't tell other reporters," Bucky explained. "But can I write about it? Not as long as you cover City Hall. Kelvin visits an old folks home for a little good P.R., maybe I can write about that. He introduces a bill regulating nursing homes and you write about it. Is that fair?"

"Hell," I said. "Life ain't fair."

"You're the original one tonight, ain't you?" Bucky asked. "Life ain't fair. Like I ain't heard that a million times since I was knee-high to a grasshopper."

I shrugged since there really wasn't any come back and we drank in silence for a few minutes. Bucky finally broke the silence.

"So Kelvin calls me this morning, says he wants to meet me. I say, you want to talk about old times, that's fine with me, I've got nothing better to do these days. He says no, he's got something important to discuss — something he saw in the paper — and could I meet him for lunch."

"Did you?"

"Did I what?"

"Meet him for lunch?"

"I went to the restaurant — Greta's over on Fifth — and waited nearly an hour for him to show. He doesn't show, so I call his office. The secretary says he's not in and she doesn't expect him back for the rest of the day. I figure he's tied up in traffic maybe, so I wait another half hour and still he doesn't show. I've got a deadline on a feature about an old guy who collects World War II mementos and I can't wait no longer," Bucky said. "With this damn arthritis I can't type too fast any more and I figure I need an extra hour or so to pound out this feature."

"So Kelvin missed lunch."

"Yeah. An hour and a half of my day shot and I didn't get a free lunch." Bucky's bourbon-and-rye was dangerously close to empty and he signaled for the bartender. "After I finish the feature, I'm thinking about this. Kelvin never missed an appointment in his life. I figure something's up and I tell Silverman about it. He tells me Kelvin's senile and probably can't tell time to save his ass."

"So what did you do about it?"

"I came over here and started drinking," Bucky said.

"To clear your mind?"

"It's clear enough to be sitting here telling you all about it."

"You really think there's a story in a missed luncheon appointment?"

"Look, Fox," Bucky said. "Kelvin and me used to be like this." He crossed his fingers. "We couldn't have been any closer without sleeping together."

"And did you?"

"What?"

"Sleep together?"

"You pig," Bucky said.

"Politics does make strange bedfellows." I emphasized the fellows.

"Kelvin wanted to talk, and he wanted to talk to me. It had to be important or he wouldn't have called. Not after all this time. Not after I stopped covering City Hall. There's a story here and it's a big one and I'm going to break it loose."

"So why are you telling me about it?"

"I need your help."

"You want *me* to help *you* get *my* job?"

"I don't want your job," Bucky insisted. "I just want one last shot at the big time."

"Like George Foreman."

"Hell, yes, like George Foreman. Put me in the ring with a story like this and let me start punching and, by God, you'll have a winner."

"And the story is that the Alderman missed lunch?"

"Oh, screw off, Fox. If you don't want to help, you don't have to." He finished his drink. "You can call me that cab now."

I had the bartender hand me the phone and I dialed a familiar number. After I hung up, I turned to Bucky. "The cab'll be in here in about ten minutes. You want to wait outside, get some fresh air?"

I helped Bucky off the stool and he leaned against me as we made our way through the bar and out the door. Outside, a slow breeze crawled through the city streets, rearranging some of the heat. We didn't talk again until a Yellow Cab pulled to the curb across the street.

"I'll show you," Bucky said as he stepped off the curb between two parked cars. "I'll show you how a reporter digs out a story."

He turned away from me and began staggering toward the cab. He'd made it almost to the center line when a dark blue Lincoln Town Car came speeding down the street.

I yelled and ran between the parked cars, but I was too late. The Lincoln struck Bucky and tossed him into the air like a rag doll. The car turned the corner and disappeared into the night before I reached Bucky.

I crouched over his body, feeling for a pulse on one wrist and then the other.

"Worm food."

I looked up to see the cab driver standing over me. He had a three-day growth of beard and a four-day lack-of-bath odor.

"He's worm food," the cabbie said. "There's nothing you can do for him now."

I stood and pulled out my notebook, a long, narrow pad I carried inside my jacket pocket.

"I called it in the moment I saw it happen," the cabbie said. "Should be a couple of cops and an ambulance along any minute now."

We could already hear the sirens.

Behind me, the reporters began pouring out of deComposing Room. One of them hustled across the street and a few minutes later he returned with Charlie Marotta, one of the newspaper's photographers.

While I spoke to the first uniformed officer on the scene, Charlie took pictures. It isn't often a newspaper reporter *is* the news.

"What's your name?" the cop asked. His closely cropped gray hair made his head appear bullet-shaped, and his thick torso strained the buttons of his uniform.

"Fox," I said. "Dan Fox. Just Dan. No middle initial."

"And the dead guy?"

"Benjamin 'Bucky' Weaver." As we spoke, I read the cop's nametag and jotted his name and badge number into my notebook.

"Okay, Just Dan," the cop said. "What happened?"

I made the story short and sweet. "Bucky had had a bit to drink so I phoned for a cab to take him home. He was crossing the street when a car came out of nowhere and ran him down."

"Where's the car now?"

"Gone," I said. "Hit-and-run."

"Make, model, any distinguishing features?"

"A dark blue Lincoln Town Car, nothing special about it."

"License plate?"

"Didn't see it."

"He's pretty near the center line. The car clip him?"

"Hit him square in the grill."

"Driving down the middle of the road, or did the car swerve?"

I thought about it for a moment. "I think it swerved. I can't be certain."

Charlie snapped a photo of me talking to the cop, momentarily blinding me with the flash.

"You a reporter?"

"Yeah," I said. "So's Bucky."

The cop looked down at the Bucky's body straddling the yellow center stripe in the road. "Looks like he's on a deadline."

The cop laughed at his own joke, but I didn't.

There was nothing else I could do for Bucky and the cop didn't have any more questions. I walked over to the cab, copied the cabbie's name and license number into my notebook, then headed inside the newspaper building and took the elevator upstairs.

The room was nearly deserted and none of the three people working the late shift spoke to me as I made my way to my desk and booted up my computer. A lot had changed over the years. Manual typewriters had given way to electric, electric typewriters had given way to dumb computer terminals, and dumb computer terminals had given way to networked personal computers. I had a hard time keeping pace with the changes and the fact that guys like Bucky had made each of the transitions continued to amaze me.

As soon as the computer finished booting up, I opened a new file and wrote a short piece about the hit-and-run that had ended Bucky's life. Next, I accessed the standing obit files we keep on all the newspaper's reporters, opened up Bucky's file, filled in the date of his death, and then read what someone else had written about him.

It was a damned shame that a man's life could be summed up in a dozen sentences, but everything seemed to be there. He had twice been nominated for the Pulitzer Prize, though he'd never received it; he'd been married once, though he'd outlived his wife and they'd had no children; and he had been a Shriner for more than half his life, dressing as Bucky the Clown for the amusement of young and old alike.

After I closed the obit file, I sent both files over the network to the copy editor's computer. Later, the copy editor would review them for grammar, spelling, and style, then queue the files up for the page layout editors who would use one or both stories in the next edition.

Before I shut down my computer, I phoned home and told Janet I was on my way. I'd seen a lot of people die over the years, but watching a hit-and-run driver kill Bucky had reminded me of my own mortality. I knew when I finally made it home, I'd have to tell Janet how much she meant to me and how glad I was that she was a part of my life.

2

AT 7:20 the next morning, the police towed a dark blue Lincoln Town Car out of the Mississippi River, Alderman William Kelvin still seated behind the wheel. He had a single bullet hole in the back of his head and Charlie Marotta snapped two dozen good photos of the Alderman before the police shooed him away.

I didn't know anything about the Alderman's late-night drive into the river until I arrived at the newspaper a few minutes past eight. Silverman called me into his office and told me all about it.

"I've got an obit on file," I told him. "We could do maybe a half page with photos."

"This is front page stuff," Silverman said. "Blood and politics always go together well. We can use the obit on an inside page, but I need the goods for page one."

While we spoke, Charlie tapped on the door and Silverman waved him in. The photographer laid a series of proof sheets on Silverman's desk and the three of us looked them over.

Kelvin had been a handsome young man when he'd first been elected to office and even in death he had maintained a certain dignity.

Still, dead is dead. Silverman circled two photos — one of the car rising from the water, the other a close-up of the alderman slumped over the steering wheel — and instructed Charlie to provide blow-ups ASAP.

"Front page, above the fold," Silverman told me after Charlie hustled out of the room. "Give me something juicy."

I returned to my desk and let my fingers do the walking through my Rolodex. I placed my first call to Detective Ballany and, after an eternity on hold, he came on the line.

"You call just to chat?" Ballany asked after I'd identified myself.

I told him what I was after.

"Maybe you're in luck," he said. "I've just been assigned the case."

"So talk to me." We'd worked together once before on a case that shook the very foundation of the city's political system and we knew we could trust one another.

"Single shot, back of the head, appears to be a .22. He died before his car went into the river, but we're waiting on the coroner's report before any of this can be confirmed."

"Any suspects?"

"Pretty much any Republican in the city."

We both laughed. Kelvin had been a die-hard Democrat.

"What about motive?"

"It wasn't a robbery or a car-jacking," Ballany said. "The Alderman still had his wallet with a couple hundred dollars in it, a Rolex worth at least a month's salary, and a diamond pinky ring."

"A mob hit?" I suggested.

"Not likely. They've been pretty quiet the past year and this just doesn't fit the pattern unless they brought in outside help."

"So where's that leave the investigation?"

"At the very beginning."

"Meaning?"

"I find out everything the Alderman did during the last twenty-four hours. I retrace every one of his steps."

"Maybe I can help."

"How's that?"

"Bucky Weaver had a luncheon appointment with the Alderman yesterday at Greta's, over on Fifth, but the Alderman never showed."

"Where's Bucky now? I need to talk to him."

"The morgue," I said. "Last night a dark blue Lincoln Town Car ran him down outside deComposing Room. I watched it happen."

There was silence on the line for a moment. Then Ballany said, "I'll have someone look at the Alderman's car, see if there's a connection. Who took the report?"

I gave him the uniformed officer's name and badge number, hung up, then returned to Silverman's office.

"I think Bucky Weaver and the Alderman are connected," I told the City Editor. "I think the Alderman's car was used to run Bucky down."

"Bucky came in here yesterday with some crack-pot story about the Alderman missing lunch."

"That's what I'm talking about," I said. "When Bucky and I were drinking last night he told me all about it."

"What was to tell?"

"Not a hell of a lot," I said, "but Bucky'd been a reporter his entire life. He smelled a story and we didn't believe him just because he's old. Imagine what we're going to feel like when that happens to us."

"Won't happen," Silverman said.

"Why's that?"

"I plan to retire before they kick my ass out."

"Not me," I said. "I'm just like Bucky. I've got ink for blood."

"Okay, Bucky Junior, you tell me what all this means. We've got a dead reporter, a dead alderman, and a missed luncheon engagement."

"I don't know yet," I said. "I'll find out."

I stood.

"Make it soon," Silverman said. "We're coming up on deadline."

I returned to my desk, booted up my computer, and pounded out a dozen paragraphs about the alderman's death. I phoned Charlie Marotta in the darkroom to ask him a few questions about that morning's events by the river, and then expanded the story by another two paragraphs.

I didn't include anything in the initial story about Bucky Weaver, leaving the two short pieces I'd prepared the night before as sufficient evidence of his passing.

I called downstairs to the newspaper's morgue and asked for everything they had on the alderman. Even though the newspaper had embraced the electronic age, very little information more than five years old had been added to the database. Everything else still existed on printed copies or on microfilm.

A few minutes later I saw Steven Harris enter the city room and I motioned him over. Silverman had given the kid a break after Michael O'Shea retired and had assigned him to the police beat. He'd gotten pretty damned jaded after that.

"What have you got on Alderman Kelvin?"

"They're not talking to me," Harris said.

"Why's that?"

"Nobody owes me," Harris said.

"So who've you been talking to?"

"Detective Ballany, his Lieutenant, the Press Officer."

"Start lower," I suggested. "Talk to the first officer on the scene. He's probably a beat cop who doesn't get his name in the papers often enough. Make his family proud if he gets a mention."

Harris looked a question at me.

"Make friends with all the uniforms you can," I said. "Some of them get promoted and when they do, they'll remember you."

"I'll see what I can do."

"And remember to share," I explained. "I've got this same story from the other side. We're going to need each other."

"Sure thing," Harris said.

I turned to my Rolodex as Harris returned to his desk, and I thumbed through all the business cards and hastily written phone numbers until I found one for Greta's. I knew the maitre d' and wanted to talk to him about the previous day's reservation. When I called the restaurant, though, the woman who answered told me that Eddie hadn't come in yet and that she'd give him a message for me.

Next, I phoned the coroner's office but I couldn't get any information from the officious dweeb who answered, nor would the police officers at the impound lot tell me anything about the alderman's car. Finally I decided that I needed to wear down a little shoe leather. I slipped my jacket on, made sure my notebook was still tucked into the pocket, and walked to City Hall.

I found Alderman Kelvin's secretary sitting at her desk staring blindly at the wall.

"Marcia," I said softly.

When she didn't respond, I gently touched her shoulder. She looked up at my face, recognized me, and then began to cry.

"I just found out," she said. "I just found out."

I held her while she sobbed, not knowing what else to do. Ten minutes passed before she regained control of herself.

"I'm sorry," she said. "Really I am. Look what I've done to your suit." She indicated the tear stains on my shoulder.

"Nothing that dry cleaning can't get out," I said, smiling.

"I've been with the alderman ten years now," she said. "After my husband died I went to secretarial school and the alderman hired me the same day I graduated. I've been here ever since. I don't know what I'll do now."

Before she could start crying again, I asked, "Tell me about yesterday."

"Yesterday was like any other day."

"How's that?" I had my notebook out and I thumbed it open to a blank page.

"The alderman came in at eight. He's always here at eight, never early and never late." She smiled at her rhyme. "I get here around 7:30 so I can have his coffee ready and the lights on and everything."

"So he shows up at eight," I prompted.

"Eight o'clock sharp. He comes in, says good-morning, and goes into his office. I follow with his coffee and the morning paper. He thanks me, compliments me on my new earrings — he always noticed things like that, not many men do — and I returned to my desk."

"And?"

"I don't talk to him again for twenty minutes or so. He buzzes me on the intercom and asks for Bucky Weaver's phone number. I tell him, he thanks me, and that's it. I see his phone line light up a moment later and I figure he's calling Mr. Weaver himself."

"Did he place all of his own calls?"

"Not usually," Marcia said. "Only personal calls."

"So you figure his call to Bucky was personal?"

"Had to be," she said. "Mr. Weaver hasn't been a political reporter for a long time. He's stuck writing about retirees."

I didn't tell her that Bucky had written his last feature the day before. I figured she'd find out soon enough.

"Any idea what they talked about?"

"I haven't a clue," Marcia said. "The line was busy for maybe three minutes, then again around ten for another few minutes. I didn't see the alderman until he came out of his office, told me he would be away from the office the rest of the day, and left."

"What happened later?"

"What do you mean?"

"You hear from Bucky later that day?"

"Sure. Around noon Mr. Weaver phones and says the alderman is late for their luncheon engagement. I didn't know anything about it so I just told Mr. Weaver that the alderman had stepped out and that I didn't expect him back."

I closed my notebook, thanked Marcia, and stood. As I reached for the door to let myself out, I had a thought. I turned back and asked, "What paper did you give the alderman yesterday?"

"Yours," she said. "The morning edition."

"Have you still got it?"

"No, the alderman took it with him when he left yesterday."

I thanked her again, and then let myself out. As I walked down the corridor I wondered what the alderman might have seen in the newspaper that would prompt him to telephone an old friend like Bucky Weaver.

I STOPPED AT a corner diner for a cup of coffee and a bagel with cream cheese, and then I returned to the office. I found a copy of the previous day's morning edition and took it back to my desk where I could spread it out. I didn't see anything significant. The president had announced a new foreign trade policy, there were uprisings in the Middle East, and another sports hero had been busted for cocaine possession. Train wrecks, plane wrecks, and automobile accidents filled the inside pages. Natural disasters across the globe filled numerous column inches. Restaurant reviews, movie reviews, and book reviews. The editorial and op-ed pages were filled with the vitriol of columnists both liberal and conservative. And in among everything else were the ads. It had been a small edition, only 96 pages, but I saw nothing unusual.

I folded the paper in half and stuffed it into my desk drawer just before a kid from the newspaper's morgue dropped off a two-inch-thick folder of information about Alderman Kelvin.

3

I SPENT THE next hour thumbing through the information about the alderman. Prior to seeking office, Kelvin had been a partner at Anderson, Kline, and Myers, a small but respected law firm that had since become one of the city's three most prestigious law firms. He took a leave of absence to run for city council the first time and, after winning the election with nearly three-quarters of the vote, he never looked back.

I found photos of Kelvin with this senator and that congressman, chairing sub-committees on public safety and urban blight. He gave lectures at the Rotary Club and the League of Women Voters, and sometimes served as a guest lecturer at the local colleges. His public views were generally moderate and his voting record seemed to emphasize a connection with the average working stiff. He usually voted against tax increases, but favored spending more money on education; he favored tax breaks to businesses, but only when they brought more jobs into the area; he always spoke out against crime, and his voting record indicated a willingness to spend money to improve the police department.

In his fifty years on the city council, Alderman Kelvin had never been involved in a scandal. I finally closed the folder and whistled softly. The alderman was like Ivory soap: he was 99 and 44/100ths percent pure. It was my job to find the impure part that had led to his death.

I slipped the folder into my top drawer along with the previous day's paper, thinking I'd take both home with me at the end of the day and spread everything over the dining room table while I looked for connections.

As I closed the drawer, my phone rang. On the other end of the line was Eddie, the maitre d' from Greta's. We exchanged greetings and chit-chat about the weather. Then I asked him, "Who made Alderman Kelvin's lunch reservation yesterday?"

"He did," Eddie answered. "I took the call myself."

"Isn't that unusual?"

"In what way?" Eddie asked.

"Wouldn't his secretary normally take care of his reservations?"

"Usually, she did, but not always," Eddie responded. "The alderman would phone in three or four times a year."

"Any pattern to his phoning?"

"You mean, was it always for lunch with the same party? No. No pattern that I ever noticed," Eddie said. "I just figured his secretary had stepped out or had the day off is why he handled it himself."

I thanked Eddie for his time, promised I'd be in for lunch some day soon, and disconnected the line. Then I called Maria and asked her about the alderman's phone calls the previous day.

"Just the two," she insisted. "Unless he placed calls while I was out of the office."

"How long were you out?"

"Ten minutes or less," she said. "I went down the hall to the supply room for some printer ribbons and paper clips. I stopped to talk to Andrea Wilson, Alderman Smith's secretary, on the way back."

"What'd you talk about?"

"We'd planned to go to lunch together and I just stopped by to confirm with her. It turned out she couldn't go and we had to reschedule."

I thanked Marcia and, after ending the call, phoned Detective Ballany and told him what I'd learned.

"I've already got the MUDs," he said. Message Unit Directories are kept by the telephone company and provide a complete list of all telephone calls from any particular number, including calls that weren't completed. "The MUDs only record external calls so the alderman could have phoned every number inside City Hall without us knowing. He made three calls yesterday morning — to Bucky, to Greta's, and to a pay phone at the airport."

"A wrong number?"

"Couldn't be," Ballany said. "He spoke for eight minutes."

"Who would he talk to at the airport?"

"Damn near anybody," Ballany said. "And we're not likely to find witnesses, either. You know how many people travel up and down that concourse every day?"

I couldn't even venture to guess.

"Thousands," Ballany said, answering his own question.

"It had to be somebody he knew," I suggested.

"We're already checking on that," Ballany said. "None of the other aldermen were scheduled to fly out of town yesterday. We're checking with his relatives now."

"Let me know how it turns out."

"I'll tell you what I can," Ballany said.

After I hung up the phone, I pushed myself out of my chair and walked over to the City Editor's office. I rapped on Silverman's door, and then pushed it open when I heard him invite me in.

I dropped into a chair across from him. Before I could open my mouth, Silverman said, "I read your piece on the alderman. Good stuff. What have you got for a follow-up?"

"Nothing significant." I told him everything I'd learned, including the information about the alderman's third phone call that morning.

"You following up on it?"

"As best I can," I said. I rubbed at my temples, trying to keep a headache from fully forming.

"So what brought you in here?" Silverman asked.

"Bucky. He was one of us," I said. "I know he hadn't been with this paper for long, but he deserves more than two inches of obituary."

"We'll kick a few thousand dollars into the dead journalists' fund and see if we can get a scholarship named after him over at the college."

"What about his funeral? Who's making the arrangements?"

"Some clown from the Shiners," Silverman said. "And I don't mean that as an insult, either. Some guy calls up, tells me he and Bucky used to do a lot of benefit gigs together at the children's hospital, and asked if I minded if he took care of the arrangements."

"So what's the plan?"

"There's a viewing this afternoon and a graveside service tomorrow. He's supposed to call me back later with the details. I'll post something over by the water cooler so everybody knows."

"Thanks," I said. Then I stood and stepped toward the door.

Before I could leave, Silverman stopped me. "Let's nail the bastard who killed Bucky."

I smiled. "The power of the press," I said, "where the pen is mightier than the Lincoln Town Car."

BACK AT MY desk I made a few phone calls to other city officials, looking for a follow-up story on the dead alderman. At times like this most politicians commend the dead on his voting record or his dedication to duty or his sterling character, and I didn't hear anything out of the ordinary from the people I contacted. Still, it was enough to cobble together a follow-up about a grieving city.

I phoned the alderman's wife and was surprised when she answered the phone. I identified myself and her voice seemed to brighten.

"Didn't we meet last Christmas at the Ball for the Homeless?" she asked. "You were with a young woman named Janet."

"That was me," I told her.

"My husband always spoke highly of you," she said. "I think he trusted you not to misquote him."

"Thank you," I told her.

"Not like some of the other reporters," she said. I could tell her attention was drifting even before she said, "I'm sorry, I've taken some medication to steady my nerves and I don't seem to be paying enough attention. Why is it that you phoned?"

"I just wanted to ask you about yesterday," I said. "Did the alderman seem upset about anything?"

"My husband was never one to become agitated by the day-to-day aggravations that seem a part of our lives," she said. "Yesterday morning he drank his orange juice, ate his bran muffin, kissed me good-bye, and left home promptly at 7:25, just as he's done every weekday morning for fifty years." She paused. "That isn't quite true," she said. "Fifty years ago he didn't need bran muffins. His breakfast back then consisted of two eggs — sunny-side up — and dry toast."

A recitation of the alderman's breakfast menu hadn't been the reason for my call, but I listened politely until she stopped. Then I asked, "So there was nothing different about yesterday?"

"Only that my husband never returned home."

That was a pretty damned significant difference, but I didn't tell her that. "I'm sorry to have bothered you Mrs. Kelvin," I said, "but if you think of anything would you give me a call?"

I waited while she found a pencil and a pad of paper, then I gave her both my work number and my home number.

After I hung up but before I could dial again, Silverman came out of his office. As he passed my desk, he said, "Here're the details on the arrangements for Bucky."

I followed him to the corkboard next to the water cooler where he posted a single sheet of white paper. I copied down the name and address of both the funeral home where the viewing had been arranged and the site of Bucky's burial the next day.

After checking the time Silverman had posted for the viewing, I glanced at my watch. I still had three hours of work to accomplish before I needed to leave for the viewing, so I returned to my desk and picked up the phone.

4

THE NEXT FEW hours passed quickly. I wrapped up a story I'd started the day before about Alderman Rizzo's attempts to expand his power base within the city's political system, and I made a few notes on a follow-up story about the effects of the recently passed no smoking ordinance that had city employees up in arms. Then I gathered up my things, including the day-old newspaper and the folder from the newspaper's morgue, figuring to stop by Bucky's viewing on my way home.

Steven Harris stopped me at the elevator as I was headed out. He said, "I talked to the beat cop like you suggested, the one who first responded to the call about Alderman Kelvin's car in the river."

"And?" I asked.

"The alderman didn't drive the car into the river."

I figured that was pretty obvious, but I let the kid tell the story his way.

"Officer Garcia said the keys weren't even in the ignition when they pulled out the car, so he figures somebody propped the alderman behind the wheel and then pushed the car down the hill there at Laclede's Landing."

"The car had to be going a pretty good clip to bounce over all the cobblestones and into the water," I said.

"The river's abnormally high this time of year," Harris explained.

"The tires may never have touched the cobblestones along the river-front."

"You get anything else from him?"

"Only an offer of additional information if anything comes his way," Harris said. "You were right about the beat cops. Nobody ever talks to them and this guy opened up like a sunflower at noon."

I clapped Harris on the shoulder and thanked him. Even if he'd never be a Michael O'Shea, he was a good kid with potential. "You learn anything else about this case, you let me know, okay?"

Harris said he would, and then we parted company. He headed into the city room and I stepped into the elevator for the ride downstairs. Charlie Marotta was already inside. He had three cameras and a camera bag draped around his neck and he was digging through the camera bag looking for something.

Without looking up, Marotta asked, "You going to this thing for Bucky?"

"On my way now," I told him.

"Yeah, me too," Marotta said. "Silverman wants some photos, maybe catch some corrupt politico trying to slip a ring off Bucky's finger."

Marotta finally stopped digging through the camera bag and he pulled out a thin black tie. After we stepped off the elevator, he stopped long enough to put it on, and then he ran his fingers through his hair and tried to smooth it into place. He asked, "How do I look?"

"Charlie," I told him. "You've never looked good."

"Right," he said as he took a quick inventory of his equipment. "Ride with you? My car's in the shop again."

The trip to the funeral home took less than ten minutes and Marotta spent most of the time complaining about his ex-wife, a woman he con-stantly referred to as "the first bitch," seeming to imply that he planned to marry a second time. As I pulled into the funeral home's parking lot, Marotta asked, "And what about Janet? You ever plan to pop the ques-tion?"

"Things are fine the way they are," I told him.

"So you're not planning on buying the cow as long as the milk's free?"

I glanced at him. I didn't have to explain my love life to Marotta, but I felt the need to respond appropriately. I gave him the finger.

Then I parked the car, we both climbed out, and we headed into the funeral home. Two beefy Shriners wearing fezzes met us at the door and requested that we sign the guest registry. On the page I signed I saw the signatures of the mayor, two aldermen, a prominent lawyer, and a half dozen names I didn't recognize.

Once inside the room, Charlie and I parted company. He began snapping photos while I circulated among the group of people who'd come to pay their respects. I nodded at the mayor and some of the other familiar faces and soon found myself standing next to the open casket and looking down at Bucky.

"He's never looked better," said a gravely voice to my left.

I looked up to find a slim man in a fez standing next to me.

"Twenty years I've known Bucky and he's never looked better," he said. "It's a damned shame, isn't it?"

"You some kind of clown?" I asked.

The slim guy introduced himself. "Jerry Throckmorton," he said as he extended his hand. "Bucky and I performed together regularly."

"I never knew Bucky was a Shriner," I said. "He never mentioned it."

Throckmorton shrugged. "Some guys flaunt it, some guys don't. Bucky was always more interested in helping the kids than in any other part of the organization. Especially the kids in the burn ward."

"Why the burn ward?" I asked.

Throckmorton shrugged. "But I've been talking with the people at the hospital. I think they've decided to rename the ward to the Bucky Weaver Burn Center for Children. The guys and I have already collected ten thousand dollars. We figure a few hundred for the plaque and the rest for some new equipment."

"You still taking donations?" I asked.

"Sure," Throckmorton said. "Those kids need all the help they can get."

I pulled out my checkbook, asked who to make it out to, then handed Throckmorton a check for $500.00. He glanced at the figure on the check before folding it up and slipping it into his breast pocket.

"That's awfully generous of you," he said as we moved away from the casket to give other mourners a chance to see Bucky in repose.

"I'd like to talk with you later," I said. "Maybe learn more about Bucky for a follow-up story in the paper. Where can I reach you?"

Throckmorton and I exchanged business cards, and then parted company when the mayor drew me aside.

Speaking softly so only I could hear his voice, the mayor said, "I heard through the grapevine that Weaver and Kelvin's deaths might be connected. You hear anything about it?"

"I'm working that angle already."

"And if they are?"

"Front page."

The mayor hesitated for a moment. "Anybody else working this angle?"

"One of the television stations maybe, but I haven't heard a thing."

"If you tie them together, could you let me know before the story runs?"

"What's your special interest, Mr. Mayor?"

"I knew both of them a long time," he explained. "They were my friends. That's all."

One of the aldermen pulled the mayor away before I could ask another question and by then Marotta had completely circled the room. He approached me.

"Get any good shots?" I asked.

"A few," he said. "Nothing special."

"A lot of people are streaming through to pay their respects," I said.

"Nobody stays long, though," Charlie said. "Might be different if he had a wife or some children to comfort."

Just then a dark-skinned nurse pushed a heavily bandaged little girl in a wheelchair up to the casket and the little girl placed a teddy bear inside with Bucky.

I glanced over at Marotta and said, "I think Bucky had a lot of children."

I ARRIVED HOME two hours later and dropped the day-old newspaper and the folder full of clips about Alderman Kelvin's career on the dining room table. Janet heard me and stepped out of the kitchen.

"You hungry?" she asked.

Instead of answering, I gathered her into my arms and kissed her long and deep and hard.

When I finally let her come up for air, Janet asked, "Still confronting your own mortality?"

"I went to the funeral home to see Bucky," I told her. "And Kelvin will probably be planted in the next few days. That's two people I've known for a long time and they're both gone now."

Janet held my hands and looked up at me.

"And then Marotta asked me a question today that got me thinking."

"What'd he ask?"

"That's not important," I said. "What's important is that you understand how much I love you."

"I do understand that," Janet said. "I've never doubted it."

I kissed her again, feeling her body press against mine as our kiss lengthened. Before long, she took my hand and led me upstairs to the bedroom.

5

I arrived at my desk the next morning without the newspaper and file folder I'd taken home the previous night. Janet had kept me awake well past midnight and when the second alarm clock finally managed to rouse me, I had to hurry through my morning routine. I finally rushed out of the house with a hot mug of instant coffee in one hand and my tie in the other.

Luckily, other than the drive-by shooting of a suspected crack dealer, no deaths had occurred overnight. I sat at my desk adjusting the knot of my tie while simultaneously trying to boot up my computer and read the morning edition of the newspaper.

Jonny Silverman stopped and leaned against the corner of my desk. He had a fresh cup of coffee in one hand and the building's ventilation system pushed the rising steam in my direction. He asked, "You have trouble getting to sleep last night?"

I wasn't about to tell my boss that the woman with whom I cohabitated had been insatiable. I said, "No, why?"

"Looks like you could have used a few more hours of sleep." He sipped from his coffee, and then swore when the hot liquid burned his tongue. When he finished cursing at his coffee, Silverman said, "Looks like it's going to be a busy week. Weaver's being planted this afternoon and Kelvin's viewing is tomorrow."

"Funeral?" I asked.

"Next day," he said. "In the afternoon."

The phone on my desk rang and I reached for it. Silverman hiked himself off the corner of my desk and headed toward his office.

"Fox," I said as soon as I had the handset pressed to my ear.

"This is Ballany," said the voice on the other end. "Can we meet somewhere for lunch?"

I suggested Greta's and then offered to make the reservation.

"Make it early, say eleven."

"No problem," I told him. "Is there anything special I should prepare for?"

I had the distinct that impression Ballany shrugged, even though I couldn't possibly have seen the gesture through the phone line. He said, "A good meal."

I knew Ballany had information that he couldn't give me over the phone so I stopped interrogating him. "I'll see you there at eleven."

After Ballany rang off, I flipped through my Rolodex for Greta's phone number and then let Eddie know when I'd be arriving. "And Eddie," I said, "I want something dark and out of the way."

"You've got it, Mr. Fox. Anything else?"

I told him there wasn't, and then I hung up the phone. Steven Harris had just entered the city room and I called to him.

"I've bought more damned doughnuts and coffee the past twenty-four hours," he complained as he approached my desk, "than I even knew existed."

"Finally learned how to work the beat cops?" I asked.

"These guys'll talk once you get 'em started," Harris explained. "Just my luck they didn't know squat about the Kelvin murder."

"That's okay," I told him. "Next time they might."

"I'm not really complaining," Harris said. "I've got an exclusive on that drive-by last night. The cops've already collared a suspect, but there's been no official confirmation of the arrest. Hell, I know the kid's name, age, address, and shoe size already. I'm on my way in to Silverman's office to see if he wants to go with the story before it's official."

I waved him on past my desk. The kid was about to experience his first scoop and I didn't plan to stand in his way.

The rest of the morning disappeared in a flurry of bullshit and paperwork. Payroll had screwed up my paycheck for the third week in a row and I spent far too much time trying to straighten everything out. When I finally finished with personnel and accounting, I barely had time to make it to Greta's for my meeting with Ballany.

He'd arrived only moments before me and Eddie escorted us directly to a darkened booth near the rear of the restaurant.

"I have a problem with this case," Ballany said after we'd settled into our seats and had ordered drinks and an appetizer.

"You don't think I killed this one, do you?" I asked. A year earlier, Ballany had suspected me in the murder of Alderman Franklin until subsequent events had cleared me.

"You could have pushed Weaver in front of the Lincoln," he said, "but you couldn't have done the alderman. The .22 isn't your style."

"Thanks," I said. I paused while the waiter served our drinks, then I asked, "What's the problem?"

"Kelvin's Lincoln killed Weaver, but Kelvin wasn't driving."

"How's that?"

"Estimated time of death," Ballany explained. "The coroner says the alderman was dead at least two hours before Weaver got hit. And he says Kelvin wasn't in the car when he died."

"Someone killed him," I said, "then used his car to run down Weaver, then put the alderman in the driver's seat and pushed the car into the river."

Ballany agreed with my summary. "That's how it looks."

"Suspects?"

He shook his head, and then said, "Tell me again what happened the other night."

I repeated the entire story start to finish, from the time I arrived in the bar and slipped onto the stool next to Bucky Weaver to the moment I went upstairs to the city room to file the story.

"And you never saw the driver of the car?" Ballany asked.

"A silhouette, that's all," I explained. "From the back as the car sped away."

"So how tall was the driver?"

"Well, he — or she, I suppose — could see over the steering wheel."

"Why'd you say 'she'?"

"No particular reason," I explained. "It's just that these days it isn't safe to assume anything."

Our appetizer arrived, a combination plate of battered and deep fried mushrooms, zucchini slices, and string cheese. Ballany forked a mushroom and held it near his lips. Before he took it into his mouth, he asked, "Was there anything about the silhouette to make you think it could have been a woman?"

"No," I said. "You suspect a woman?"

"His wife's alibi is weak, that's all."

"Women kill their husbands for many different reasons," I said, "but what reason would she have to kill Bucky?"

Ballany spoke around the mushroom. "No reason I can find."

The waiter returned and we ordered lunch — steak and potatoes for Ballany, breaded white fish for me. Ballany had no additional information to share so our conversation drifted elsewhere. During lunch, after I saw Ballany slather butter and sour cream all over his potatoes, I suggested he give up red meat and cut back on his cholesterol. He suggested I use my fish as an enema. By the end of the meal we'd shared our opinions on local and national politics, criminal rights, and freedom of the press. While we didn't agree on much of anything, we did agree to disagree.

When the bill came, I paid it despite Ballany's protestations. He offered to ante-up the next time we got together.

I DIDN'T HAVE time to return to the office, so I drove directly to the cemetery, arriving in time to see Bucky's casket being carried from the hearse to the graveside by six Shriners in clown suits.

Bucky Weaver's graveside service, despite the presence of half a dozen men in clown suits and three or four dozen children, all of whom appeared to have been burn victims, was a solemn occasion.

A reverend whose denomination I couldn't determine, but who seemed conservatively mainstream, spoke about Bucky for twenty minutes, then spent another fifteen minutes discussing man's place in God's world. I'm not a particularly religious man, but I found myself hoping that there was a Heaven and that Bucky was there, bellied up to the bar along with all the other journalists who'd gotten there before him.

The clowns lowered Bucky's casket into the ground and the nurse who'd accompanied three of the children stepped forward and dropped a single rose into the open grave. She was the same woman who'd accompanied the girl with the teddy bear to Bucky's viewing. There were tears on her cheeks and she used a hanky to dry them as she stepped back.

I recognized Jerry Throckmorton despite his costume and watched as he threw the first shovelful of dirt onto Bucky's casket. It landed with a hollow thud and I turned away. Grown men don't cry, but I felt my eyes begin to water and I didn't want others to see me.

AFTER THE SERVICE I drove to Bucky's apartment building. I'd never been to his place before so I didn't know what to expect. The building's superintendent unlocked the door for me after I showed him the I.D. the newspaper issues to all of its reporters.

"I'm not sure I should be doing this," he said for the third time as he pushed the door open. "Bucky wouldn't stand for having strangers goin' through his stuff."

"We worked together," I repeated. "I'm not a stranger."

"You ain't from his regular paper. You're from that 'nother one he went to work for when his paper folded."

I agreed with the superintendent's conclusion.

"Then you's a stranger."

I really didn't want to argue with the superintendent so I stepped past him and into the living room of Bucky's place. The superintendent followed right on my heels. When I stopped suddenly, he actually ran into me, and then he peered around me and whispered, "Mother of God!"

Someone had torn Bucky's place apart. The pictures had been removed from the walls, the couch and chair cushions had been torn open, the drawers in his desk opened and their contents dumped on the floor, the books pulled off of his bookshelf.

"Bucky wasn't no Martha Stewart when it come to housekeeping," said the superintendent, "but he never done nothing like this."

I stepped carefully toward the hallway. Then I turned and told the little man, "You'd better phone the police. Someone's ransacked the place."

He stepped toward the phone on the floor.

"From your place," I said. "You don't want to mess up any fingerprints."

"Of course," he said. "Of course!"

The little man bustled away, out the door and down the steps to his basement apartment. After he'd gone, I made my way down the hallway, glancing into the kitchen, the bathroom, and both bedrooms. Every room had been torn apart, every cabinet emptied, every closet cleared.

As I walked down the hall, I stepped over the scattered remains of a newspaper and the yellowing wedding photo of a black couple, the frame twisted and the glass shattered.

As I stepped into the second bedroom, I heard a sound behind me. I thought it was the superintendent returning so I didn't turn. I asked, "How long before the police arrive?"

In response, someone hit me on the back of the head. I dropped to my knees. As I fell I looked in the mirror mounted over the dresser and saw a tall, dark-haired man standing behind me. I didn't have time to memorize his features before a second blow sent me crashing face-first onto the floor.

WHEN I CAME to, I found the superintendent kneeling beside me and washing my face with a cold wet washcloth.

"I was afraid you wasn't comin' to," he said. "You was out like a light."

"The police?" I mumbled.

"Any minute now," he said.

I tried to sit up.

"Don't you be moving now," he said. "They's blood coming from back of your head. I ain't no damned doctor can fix you up none, so you just stay put till somebody come to help."

I groaned but didn't move. The cold cloth on my forehead felt so good, I just closed my eyes and waited. When I opened my eyes a second time, I found myself looking at the highly polished shoes of a uniformed police officer. He was speaking into a walkie-talkie, calling for an ambulance.

When he finished, he squatted down beside me. "Can you talk?"

"Sure," I said.

"What happened?"

I told him.

"Can you describe the guy?"

"Six foot, give or take," I said.

"Give or take what?"

"Two inches maybe."

"And?" he prompted.

"Dark hair. Black or dark brown."

"Curly or straight?"

I thought hard for nearly a minute. "Wavy."

"Caucasian, Black, Oriental, Hispanic?"

"Caucasian," I said. "Ruddy skin."

"Eyes?"

"Two," I said.

"I mean, what color?"

I didn't know so I shook my head. That was a mistake because my head starting pounding.

"What was the guy wearing?"

"Jeans. T-shirt. Shirt was white with a pocket."

"Anything else? Scars, tattoos, anything?"

"Nothing," I said. "Nothing at all."

The superintendent stood just outside the bedroom door talking to the other cop. I couldn't hear everything they said, but the little guy kept repeating, "I didn't see a thing. When I come back up here, he was just laying there on the floor. I done the best I could, got him a cold washrag and all."

"You're sure?" the cop kept asking.

"Sure I'm sure. I don't look like I'm sure? Of course I'm sure. Twenty-five years I been the super here and I never seen nothing like this before."

The arrival of two Emergency Medical Technicians with a stretcher interrupted their circular conversation. The two EMTs worked me over and then loaded me onto the stretcher. As they were wheeling me from the apartment, I stopped them and motioned for the building's superintendent to step closer.

"'Preciate what you did," I said hoarsely. I handed him my card. "Call that number," I instructed. "Ask for Jonny Silverman and tell him what happened. Okay?"

The little guy nodded.

"Soon as you can get to a phone," I insisted.

Instead of Jonny Silverman, though, Detective Ballany met me at the hospital.

"Bucky Weaver's was our next stop," he told me. "We found a torn piece of his jacket caught in the grill of the alderman's Lincoln."

"The two are connected?" I asked.

"Intimately," Ballany said.

Jonny Silverman arrived just as Ballany finished up, and Janet stepped into the room a moment later. She squeezed between the two men and sat beside me on the bed. She took one of my hands between both of hers and stared deep into my eyes.

"Are you okay?" she asked.

"Of course," I lied. My head hurt like hell.

Ballany pointed a finger at me and cocked his thumb back. "I'll leave you all alone," he said before stepping out of the room.

Janet turned to Silverman. "What story have you got him working on this time?"

"Alderman Kelvin."

"It figures," she said. "Every time there's a dead alderman, Dan gets the assignment."

"I cover City Hall," I told her. "Who else would get it?"

She didn't answer me. Instead, Janet said, "I talked to your nurse before I came in here. She said the doctor wants you to stay overnight for observation. They're worried you might have a concussion."

"I know."

"You are planning to stay, aren't you?"

Silverman answered before I could. "I'll have someone else follow up on the Kelvin story. You can pick up on things when you get out of here."

"I've got a telephone," I insisted. "I can track a few leads from here."

6

SILVERMAN LEFT JANET and me alone in the room. She still sat on the bed and continued to hold my hand. "You're going to stick with this story, aren't you?"

"Of course," I told her.

"I think my brother wanted to be you," she said. "And that's why he got killed."

We'd had this discussion before and I had the feeling we'd have it again. Every time things get a little rough, Janet reminds me of her younger brother, an intern at the newspaper until his in-depth investigation of an alderman who raped and mutilated children led to his own death.

"Billy thought it was a reporter's responsibility to expose all the evil in the world. He thought reporters were gods, standing above everybody else and looking down, but reporters are just like everybody else," Janet said. "They bleed."

I tried to smile. "I know."

She squeezed my hand, then leaned forward and kissed me lightly on the lips. Just then an aide stepped into the room and interrupted us.

"How are you feeling, Mr. Fox?" the aide asked.

"With my fingers, mostly." Neither Janet nor the aide laughed at my joke, so I shrugged and said, "Except for a splitting headache, I'm fine."

"The doctor has you on a mild pain killer," the aide said. "You should begin feeling better soon."

Janet moved out of the way so the aide could take my temperature and blood pressure, and then resumed her place on the bed beside me as soon as the aide left us alone again.

"I looked through the files you left on the dining room table," Janet said.

"And?"

"Kelvin was a straight arrow, wasn't he?"

"Seems that way," I said. "I never heard of, nor reported a scandal that had his fingerprints on it."

"Isn't that some kind of a contradiction?" Janet asked.

"What?"

"An honest politician," she said. "Politicians must face an awful lot of temptation. Everybody wants a favor or some kind of special consideration, and some people are willing to pay for it."

I agreed with her.

"So either Kelvin really was clean, or he was one of the best there is at hiding his dirt." Janet paused and thought for a moment. "You think Bucky had something on him?"

"Like what?"

Janet shrugged. "I was thinking, though, that the clips you brought home were all from your paper, but Bucky was covering City Hall while you were still in diapers. Doesn't your morgue have anything from the other newspaper, something with Bucky's byline on it?"

"I'll ask," I said. "Hand me the phone."

Janet didn't move. "Do it tomorrow. Tonight you need to rest."

I tried to roll over and reach for the phone myself. Janet stood, then moved the phone as far away from me as the cord would allow.

"That isn't fair," I told her.

"You need your rest," she insisted. "I won't stop you from going back to work tomorrow, but tonight you're just going to relax."

Janet fell asleep in the visitor's chair long before I did and the day shift nurse woke us both the next morning. A few minutes later the doctor stepped into the room for a brief examination. She told me my head would continue to hurt and that I should stop by her office in two weeks to have any stitches removed that didn't fall out on their own. "Take your medicine, keep your scalp clean, and don't turn your back on strangers," she said. "Otherwise, you're free to go."

Janet helped me dress, then took me home in her car. After I showered and changed into clean underwear and a fresh suit, she drove me to Bucky's apartment complex where my car had remained overnight. I kissed her good-bye, listened to her caution me about watching my back, then I drove downtown to the newspaper building.

At my desk, after assuring Silverman that I was fit to return to work, and after explaining to half the rest of the office what had happened to me, I dialed Detective Ballany's number.

After the usual salutations and his query about my health, Ballany said, "Bucky kept a collection of his newspaper clips, apparently everything he ever had published, from the first one-paragraph obit he wrote to his most recent piece about a retired school teacher doing volunteer work with Project Literacy."

"Must have taken up a lot of space."

"An entire closet, and everything was neatly pasted into old photo albums," Ballany explained. "We've been through everything, put it all back in chronological order. There's one album missing though, maybe two. He didn't have anything for 1957."

"The entire year?" I asked.

"Gone."

"You think that's what the goon who assaulted me was after?"

"Your guess is as good as mine," Ballany insisted. "Something happened to 1957."

"Anything else missing?"

"Not that we can determine," he said. "Whoever ransacked the place did a pretty good job of it. I'm surprised the neighbors didn't hear anything, the ones that were home in the middle of the day, that is."

"Anyone see a stranger around the building about that time?"

"Only you," Ballany said, "and the postman, but we checked him out. He's the relief man on the route, covering because the regular guy had a cold."

After completing my conversation with Ballany, I called down to the newspaper's morgue and asked for copies of every story with Bucky Weaver's byline from 1957.

"He wasn't with us then, was he?" asked the voice on the other end of the line. When I told the kid in the morgue the name of the paper Bucky had been working for at the time, the kid said, "I don't think I'll find much."

"Why's that?"

"Our own stuff's in pretty bad shape that far back, and we didn't routinely save anything our competitors did."

"Is there another source?"

"When the paper finally closed its doors, they donated their files to the Journalism Department at City College. Their entire morgue is over there."

"Can you get what I need?"

"Sure," said the kid. "But I need supervisor's approval to leave the building during working hours."

"I'll take care of it, kid," I told him. A moment later I stepped into Jonny Silverman's office, told him what I needed and why, and he called the kid's supervisor directly.

After hanging up the phone, Silverman reminded me about Alderman Kelvin's viewing that afternoon. "You still plan to go?"

I told him I did.

"Then you might want to do something about that bandage," he suggested.

I went to the men's room with a pair of scissors and trimmed away as much of the bandage as I could, leaving only a patch about two inches square covering the worst of the sutured wound. Even though I wouldn't be a poster boy for good looks, at least I no longer looked like the Mummy's ugly cousin.

Back at my desk, I found a message that Alderman Rizzo had phoned, so I placed a call to his office. His secretary put me through immediately.

"I saw that hack piece you did on me yesterday," the alderman said as soon as he heard my voice. Frank Rizzo was a blue-collar guy who'd muscled his way into city politics after the death of Alderman Bill Franklin. "I ain't too happy with it."

"Can I quote you on that?" I asked.

"Look, Fox, I know you ain't too happy with the way I run my ward, but it really ain't none of your business what I do or how I do it. I got some people who like the way I do my job and that's who I'm working for. Them people."

"They wouldn't happen to be people with Mob ties, would they?" I asked.

"I represent the average joe," Rizzo said. "Mr. Blue Collar and his wife. They got a mortgage and a couple of cars and too many kids and not enough money. What I'm doing is working for them, trying to make this city a better place, better schools, more cops, more jobs."

"Is that why you voted against the recent proposal to increase the average police officer's pay by 4%?"

"I voted against it because it was a bad deal for the cops," Rizzo said. "Kelvin amended the proposal, putting a cap on the number of hours an off-duty officer could work at a part-time job. I know what kind of money some of these guys make, and a lousy 4% extra in their pay envelope every week ain't enough to cover the difference between what they'll lose from the part-time work."

"You think the police union appreciates your efforts on their behalf?"

"Damned right I do," Rizzo said. "The proposal comes up again next week. With Kelvin out of the picture I can get his amendment removed and then maybe we can get the raise pushed through."

"So Kelvin's death benefited the police department?" I asked.

"Hey," Rizzo protested. "I wasn't saying nothing like that. His death had nothing to do with the proposal or his amendment. All the cops in this city are square shooters and they wouldn't do nothing cheesy like you're suggesting."

"I'm not suggesting anything, alderman," I said. "I just asked if his death benefited the police department."

"Yeah, well you keep making cracks like that somebody's liable to be writing you a few extra parking tickets, maybe impounding your car."

I smiled. Rizzo was as easy to play as a kid's card game. If he didn't wise up soon, he wouldn't last long in city politics. I thanked him for his time and rang off.

I batted out a quick piece for the paper about the upcoming reintroduction of the proposal to increase pay for the police department, including a couple of Rizzo's comments. After I printed out a hard copy, I handed it to Steven Harris and suggested he get a few comments from cops in the street to flesh it out. He scanned what I had, then told me he'd pad it as best he could.

Then he said, "I've got a line on something you might be interested in."

"What's that?" I asked.

"The bullet that killed Kelvin," Harris said. "My source thinks he heard that it may have been fired from the same gun as one used in an open investigation."

"How far back?" I asked.

"Two, maybe three months," Harris said. "The dead guy's a wino named Jerzy Hayden, nobody knows him, nobody cares, and the investigation went cold."

"You know any more than that?" I asked.

Harris shrugged. "The guy heard a rumor is all. I can't get anyone to confirm it."

"Let me try my sources," I said.

I returned to my desk and phoned Lt. Ballany. He wasn't in so I left a message.

AT THE VIEWING for the alderman, I spotted the nurse who'd been at Bucky Weaver's funeral. She wasn't wearing her nurse whites and she wasn't accompanied by any children. I worked my way around the room until I stood next to her. After we introduced ourselves, I asked, "How did you know the alderman?"

"He put me through nursing school," Sharon Gleason explained. "Then he used his connections to get me a job at the hospital. I transferred into the children's burn ward about fifteen years ago and I've been there ever since."

"That's how you knew Bucky?"

She smiled. "Bucky was wonderful with the children. He always made them laugh. I'm really surprised he never had any of his own."

"How well did you know Bucky?"

"I guess I knew him well enough," she said. "He was a kind, gentle man."

The Mayor interrupted my conversation with Sharon Gleason, asking about the direction my recent stories on Alderman Rizzo had taken, and when I turned back to speak with Sharon again she was gone.

Ballany met me outside the funeral home a few minutes later.

"I got your message," he said. He'd been leaning against my car and he pushed himself off of it. "I've been out here for an hour. How long does it take to look at a dead guy?"

"You could have come inside and found me."

"Not interested in making nice with the politicos," Ballany said. "Makes me look like I'm polishing brass and licking boots."

I didn't say anything.

"So why'd you call?"

"Got a guy says the bullet pulled from Kelvin's brain matches one found lodged in another victim some months back. Any truth to the rumor?" I opened my car door and rolled down the window. The tail end of the heat wave still lingered over the city.

"Dead wino we just I.D.'d the other day," Ballany said.

"What ties the Alderman to the wino?"

"Another than the bullet?" Ballany asked. Then he shrugged. "Not a damned thing, far as I know."

"How'd you tumble that the two were connected?"

"Routine," Ballany explained. "I asked when was the last time we seen a body with a .22 lodged in its brain. Some yutz detective still wearing diapers tells me about this case he pulled his first week on the job. I had ballistics pull the files and they confirmed the match. Surprised the hell out me, that's for sure."

The mayor stepped out of the funeral home and a moment later his limousine pulled smoothly to the curb. Ballany and I watched as his honor settled into the car.

"Must be nice," Ballany said. "Let some other joe do the driving for you, have the air conditioning already cranked up before you even get in the car." As the mayor's limousine pulled away, Ballany turned toward me. "Unless you've got something for me, I'm headed back to the station."

As Ballany walked away, I slipped into my car and fired up the engine. A moment later, I flipped on the air conditioner and sat thinking while it slowly cooled off the interior.

7

BACK IN THE office, I discovered that the kid from the newspaper's morgue had returned from City College. He'd left a twelve-inch thick stack of copies in a folder on my desk and I began thumbing through them after I settled into my chair. I saw Bucky's byline on every story but one and in the story without his byline, he was mentioned as a Pulitzer Prize nominee for a series of articles he had written the previous year about the mob's alleged involvement with prostitution. Apparently Bucky had gone undercover — so to speak — to interview nearly two dozen women involved in the trade and his articles had contributed directly to the arrest and conviction of three pimps and a D'Angelo family cousin.

He hadn't received the award.

I skimmed the rest of the articles, quickly discovering that Bucky had been a general assignment reporter back in the mid-fifties, covering whatever his editor assigned to him. I waded through any number of stories about meetings, tragedies ranging from automobile wrecks to suicides to warehouse fires, and one particularly cute Valentine's Day piece about a newlywed couple who had gone steady in high school but had lost contact with one another until their high school's fiftieth reunion.

I'd finished looking through all the stories Bucky had written in 1957 and was closing the folder when Silverman came out of his office and motioned to me. I pushed myself out of my seat and crossed the room to his office.

"I just got a call from Alderman Rizzo," Silverman said after he'd settled back into his chair.

"And?" I asked as I dropped into the one chair Silverman kept in his office for visitors

"He wants your beat changed. He thinks maybe you'd be better off covering the city pound." Silverman shook his head. "The schmuck hasn't even completed his first term and already he thinks he has weight to throw around."

"He'll hang himself in no time," I said. "He hasn't got the staying power a guy like Kelvin had. Kelvin always played it straight, played it smart, and played it for the long term."

"So what have you got on Kelvin?" Silverman asked.

"Everybody loved the man," I said. "Not an enemy in the world."

"His death wasn't random," Silverman said. "Neither was Bucky's."

"I know it," I told my boss, "but I can't find anybody who can figure out the connection between the two men."

"You don't find something soon this whole thing'll blow into the back pages somewhere," Silverman said. "I want to keep this thing on the front page as long as we can."

The news media is a lot like the mortuary industry. We make our living from the tragedies of others. Most of the time it doesn't bother me because the people who suffer aren't connected to me in any way. This time, though, it was different. I'd been drinking with Bucky only minutes before his death, and I'd known the alderman for years.

Silverman pushed a piece of paper across the desk to me. I glanced at it and realized it was a press release issued by our paper.

"The college jumped on the idea," Silverman said. "The paper pledged two thousand a year and City College agreed to administer the Benjamin 'Bucky' Weaver Memorial Scholarship Fund. We're running this in the next edition."

I scanned the release, realized it didn't say anything that Silverman hadn't just told me, and I smiled. "At least something good's come out of this."

Silverman changed the subject. "You going to the alderman's funeral service?" he asked.

"Unless I get hit in the head again," I told him.

"It'll be at St. Mark's," Silverman said.

St. Mark's is the cathedral downtown near the river. The last time I'd been there two goons had caught me in the parking lot and had tried to beat the crap out of me.

Silverman continued, "There'll be television cameras, so expect to see all the local politicians and glad-handers."

"Death brings out the best in local politics," I said as I pushed myself out of the chair. I needed to make a few more calls before the funeral service.

I MADE MY calls, following up on a story I'd done the week before, and then I phoned Janet to remind her of the funeral. She wasn't in the office and her partner, a dumpy woman named Marge who could do things with a computer that I couldn't even imagine, informed me that Janet was at a client's site.

"Off-site infodump," Marge said.

I asked her to relay a message for me.

"E-mail it to her," Marge said.

Even though I use a computer every day, I hadn't mastered much beyond the word processing program I was obligated to use, and I explained that to Marge.

"Oh, all right," she said, obviously irritated. "I'll interface with Janet later and provide the data you just transmitted."

As I disconnected the phone line, the kid from the morgue stopped at my desk. "I found something else," he said. "It was on the floorboard of my car. I guess it fell out of the folder I brought over from City College."

He handed me a photocopy of a story Bucky had written. It appeared to be a follow-up story to one he'd written earlier about a warehouse fire.

"Thanks," I told the kid, and then I stuffed the copy into the folder with other stories Bucky had written in 1957. If I had time after the funeral service I hoped to spread everything out on the dining room table and see if anything in the folder containing Bucky's writing correlated with anything in the newspaper or the folder of information about Alderman Kelvin that I had left at home two nights earlier.

The phone rang. When I answered it, Janet asked, "What'd you say to piss off Marge?"

"I told her I couldn't use e-mail."

"That would do it," Janet said. "The woman thinks the entire world revolves around computers."

We both knew that was what made Marge the ideal partner for Janet.

"So what was it you wanted?" Janet asked. "I think Marge garbled the message. All it says is 'Tonight. Funeral. Going?' then your name and office number."

I told her about Kelvin's funeral. "I have to go," I said. "Thought you might want to join me."

"This a date?"

"We can make it one," I said. The suggestion wasn't as morbid as it sounded. "Dinner after. One of the Italian places on the Hill."

"I'll meet you at home," Janet said.

After exchanging a few terms of endearment, I disconnected the line and flipped open my notebook. It was similar to a steno pad, but only half as wide, with a coil of wire across the top so the pages could be flipped up and over. I'd been using one the entire time I'd been a newspaperman, and I found a certain level of comfort in knowing that in these days of computers, on-line services, and e-mail, some things never seemed to change. I'd been scribbling in this particular notebook for a couple of days now, having filled the previous notebook only a few hours before I'd walked across the street to drink with Bucky. I thumbed through the pages, scanning my scribbles and hoping that some bit of information would leap off one of the pages and lead me to Bucky's killer.

I didn't feel disappointed when I reached the last page and hadn't found anything. I'm a reporter, not a detective.

I reached for the phone and dialed Ballany's direct line. It rang six times, and then my call was switched to his voice mail. I left my name and number, then disconnected.

I stood, stretched, and crossed the city room to the coffee machine where a pair of quarters produced a lukewarm cup of weak coffee with too much sugar and not enough cream. I sipped at it on the return trip to my desk.

Charlie Marotta stepped off the elevator and crossed the room toward me. He had a half dozen proof sheets with him and he spread them across the top of my desk. He tapped his index finger on one of them and said, "You see anything common in these?"

I looked at the proof sheets, squinting to examine the black and white prints he'd made from 35mm film he'd shot at Bucky's viewing and funeral, and from the alderman's viewing.

"They had a lot of friends in common," I said a moment later.

"Politicians, mostly," Marotta said.

"That would figure. Kelvin was a politician and Bucky covered City Hall for a long time."

"What about these two?" Marotta asked. He singled out two men in their eighties, men who appeared at both viewings but not at Bucky's funeral. "I've checked around. They don't work for the funeral home, and they're not part of the mayor's entourage."

I looked a question at Marotta. I knew he was leading somewhere.

"Steve Anderson and Thomas Kline," he said. "When's the last time they were seen in public?"

I shook my head. The two surviving original partners of Anderson, Kline, and Myers had long ago stopped making public appearances and rumor had it that Kline's brain had long been on permanent vacation.

Marotta continued. "They were in and out of Kelvin's viewing before you arrived, but I caught them slipping into Bucky's viewing after everyone else had left."

"They employed Kelvin before he went into politics, but what's their connection to Bucky?" I asked.

Marotta shrugged. "I just take the pictures. It's mugs like you get to do the investigating."

I glanced at my watch, and then asked, "You covering Kelvin's funeral tonight?"

"Stiffs are my specialty," Marotta said. "Can I get a ride?"

"Not this time," I told him. "Janet's going with me. I've got to meet her at home."

Marotta scooped up the proof sheets. "Then you'd better hurry home," he said. "You won't get a good seat if you're late."

I glanced at my watch again. Marotta was right. I grabbed my notebook and slipped it into my hip pocket. Then I tucked the folder of Bucky's writing under my arm and headed out.

Steven Harris caught my elbow as I stepped off the elevator in the lobby. He pulled me to the side and whispered, "There's something going down. Yesterday all it took was a few doughnuts and some coffee and I had the beat cops talking to me about everything. Today I got zip."

"Think it's coming down from above?" I asked.

"Haven't got a clue," Harris said. "But you'd have thought I was a leper the way I was treated today."

"What were you digging for?"

"Kelvin's killer," he said, "same as you."

"Get any more on that drive-by the other night?"

"That story's old news," Harris explained. "Couple of gang-bangers having it out. Killer's already plea-bargaining. Kelvin's still the hot ticket."

"And Bucky," I said.

Harris looked at me with a puzzled expression on his face. "You actually cared for the old guy, didn't you?"

"He was one of us, kid," I said. "Don't ever forget your own."

"So how do I pry these clams open?" Harris asked. "How do you get sources to talk when they don't want to?"

"Persistence," I said. "Hard-headed persistence." I shifted the weight of the folder of Bucky's writing from one arm to the other. "You keep asking questions until somebody says something. But if they've got orders from above not to talk, most of those guys will be hard to crack."

"Don't I know it," Harris said as he shook his head.

"Keep your chin up," I said. Then I stepped away from him and headed down the hall toward the back door and the employee parking lot beyond it.

8

JANET ARRIVED HOME before I did and I parked beside her car. Once inside, I dumped the folder of Bucky's writing on the dining room table and climbed the stairs to our bedroom.

Janet had just stepped out of the shower and was toweling her hair dry in front of the bathroom mirror. Although we never discussed it, there was a good ten year difference in our ages and for just a moment I stood in the doorway admiring the swell of her hips, the fullness of her breasts, and the way her soft skin glistened with water from the shower.

Then Janet realized I was watching her and she turned toward me. "Better get going," she said. "They won't hold the funeral for us."

I peeled off my clothes and tossed them on the bed. Janet had already laid out my black suit and a starched white shirt fresh from the dry cleaners. I began changing into them.

As I bent over to pull on my pants, Janet stopped me and examined the top of my head. The two-inch square of gauze had come loose and she peeled it off to examine the sutured gash underneath.

"It's not pretty," she said.

"But it'll heal," I told her.

"Any idea who did this to you?"

"Probably the same guy who tore up Bucky's apartment."

Janet wadded up the gauze and carried it into the bathroom with her as we spoke. She returned with a damp washcloth and made me sit on the edge of the bed while she cleaned the dried blood off my scalp. When she finished, she said, "If you aren't going to shower, at least you should shave."

I ran my fingers over my chin and felt the day's growth of stubble. Then I stepped into the bathroom and plugged in the electric razor.

As I shaved, Janet stood beside me and began applying her make-up. She asked, "The police any closer to solving the murders?"

I shrugged. "Not that I can tell."

"What about you?"

"There's a story here somewhere," I explained. "Something in the past ties Bucky and Kelvin together in a way that no one would suspect. And that's why they were both killed. If I find what links the two men together will I find the killer?" I finished shaving and switched off the electric razor. "I don't know. But finding that link between them will certainly put us all one step closer."

As we finished dressing and then on the drive to the church, Janet told me about her day. Less than a year earlier she and Marge had opened a business creating web pages on the Internet. They had achieved modest success, which meant that they paid all their expenses but had yet to draw any income from the business. Janet had spent most of the afternoon trying to convince a client of his company's need for a presence on the Internet and her company's ability to provide him with a professionally designed web page.

"The man didn't know his ass from an asterisk, and he had never heard of HTML," Janet said. "He was a complete computer illiterate. It was so frustrating."

When we arrived at St. Mark's, I parked my car at the far end of the lot so it wouldn't get banged up by all the limousines pulling up in front of the cathedral. In addition to the steady stream of limousines, the parking lot quickly filled with Lincolns, Cadillacs, BMWs, and Mercedes. Scattered among the luxury cars were older American cars like mine — Chevrolets, Fords, and Dodges — belonging to the print media, city employees, and general voting population.

Camera crews from all three local television stations had parked their vans to one side of the cathedral, and I spotted a crew from CNN. I led Janet up to the church and inside the huge double doors. As we stepped inside, I felt her trembling.

I leaned over and whispered, "You okay?"

She whispered back. "I have bad feelings about this place. The last time we were here you were attacked."

"Won't happen this time," I said, and then Charlie Marotta spotted us and walked over.

"Big crowd," he said. "Everybody who's anybody is here already."

"Anderson and Kline?"

"Second row behind the widow," Marotta said. Then he showed us where the mayor and each of the aldermen were sitting. While Marotta was pointing out the movers and shakers, I spotted Marcia Jones, Kelvin's secretary; Sharon Gleason, the hospital nurse who knew both the dead alderman and the dead reporter; and Detective Ballany.

Ballany spotted us and gave us a two-finger salute. Then a uniformed officer encouraged us to take a seat because we were holding up the people behind us. Marotta slipped away and continued photographing the assembled mourners. Janet and I found a seat three pews from the rear, squeezed between a matronly woman sobbing quietly behind her veil and an elderly man who kept tapping the silver tip of his cane against the floor.

The service began a few minutes later and we sat through the entire mind-numbing event. Father Carneghi spoke, the mayor spoke, and then we listened to a virtual parade of people from Kelvin's past all talking about the multitude of good things he had done as a person and as a politician. We learned about his early years as a grade school student and we learned about his college days and his time in law school. Steve Anderson talked about Kelvin's first few years with Anderson, Kline, and Myers, and about his election to the city council in 1957. Various current and former aldermen spoke about Kelvin's years in office, and by the end of the service you would have thought Kelvin was up for sainthood.

I took notes throughout the service and then as we all streamed out of the cathedral, I stopped a number of the mourners and solicited comments. As we waited on the front steps for the pallbearers to carry the casket out of the cathedral and down the steps to the waiting hearse, I found myself standing next to Sharon Gleason. I introduced her to Janet and the two women greeted each other with the usual reserve of strangers who don't expect to see each other ever again.

A moment later the pallbearers came down the steps, slipped the casket into the hearse, and the crowd began to slip away to their individual automobiles. The widow was escorted to the limousine allotted to the family and then the hearse pulled away from the curb, the family's limousine behind it, and then the mayor's. The funeral parade wound its way out of the parking lot, past city hall, and up onto the highway for the trip to Forest Hills.

Janet and I slipped into the parade near the end of the line and, while we inched our way along, she asked, "Where'd you meet Ms. Gleason?"

"She's a nurse in the children's burn ward," I said. "I saw her first at Bucky's viewing."

"So how's she connected to the alderman?"

"He put her through nursing school."

"Why'd he do that?"

I shrugged. "He hired his secretary straight out of secretarial school after her husband died. He was always doing stuff like that."

Janet stared out the car window for a few minutes, then she said, "You said he *put* her through school?"

"Yeah."

"Like, he paid for it?"

I thought for a moment. "That's certainly the impression I got."

"You know anything else about her?"

I glanced over at Janet. "Like what?"

"She's certainly young enough to be the alderman's daughter."

"He never had children."

"Not with his wife, maybe."

"Are you suggesting?" I shook my head. "Kelvin didn't screw around."

"It only takes one time," Janet suggested. "It could have been hushed up, especially an inter-racial thing. Kelvin certainly had the money."

By then the hearse had pulled into Forest Hills. By the time we parked and walked to the gravesite, Father Carneghi was halfway through his graveside commentary and he instructed us to all bow our heads for a moment of prayer. As everyone else's head dipped down, I looked over the crowd, seeking out Sharon Gleason.

I never found her.

I did spot Steve Anderson. He was searching through the crowd the same as I was and our gazes locked for a moment. Then Father Carneghi finished his prayer and everyone else's heads rose, interrupting our stare down.

THE FUNERAL HAD caused us to miss the dinner rush, so Janet and I easily found an Italian restaurant on the Hill that wasn't crowded. We were led to a booth in the back, lit only by a flickering candle stuck in the top of an empty Chianti bottle.

We sat across from one another and tried not to talk about work. We examined the menus, ordered baked ravioli as an appetizer, two glasses of red wine to drink, and waited in silence while our wine was served.

We'd been living together since shortly after her brother's death, but we'd never made a formal commitment. Two funerals so close together had made me begin to question my mortality.

"I've been thinking," I started.

"Yes?"

The moment seemed right, the mood seemed right, but I still couldn't bring myself to do it. "That when this is over, we should get away, take some time off."

"It's not a good time for me," Janet said. "The business is just getting on its feet, we have two critical deadlines coming up, and I wouldn't want to leave Marge like that."

The entire time we had been together, it had been my deadlines interfering with our lives. Now Janet had deadlines. I shook my head.

The waiter interrupted to serve our appetizer and he asked if we were ready to order.

We were.

WHEN WE RETURNED home, I slipped off my jacket and laid it across the back of the couch. Then I loosened my tie, unbuttoned the top button of my shirt, and settled into one of the dining room chairs. As I began spreading everything I'd brought home across the table, Janet climbed the stairs.

When she returned a few minutes later, she wore a shortie robe securely fastened around her waist. I couldn't tell if she wore anything underneath it. Another night I might have tried to find out.

"What are you doing?" she asked as she rested her hands on my shoulders.

"The answer's in here somewhere," I told her, indicating the papers I'd spread across the table with a sweep of my arm. "Somewhere in all these stories. The alderman saw something in our paper the other day that made him call Bucky. The guy who clobbered me in Bucky's apartment took Bucky's clips from 1957. There's a connection. I just don't know what it is."

Janet had walked around the table as I spoke and she settled into the chair opposite me. She picked up a photocopy of an article I'd written about the alderman in the late eighties. He'd just received a Good Citizenship Award from some organization or other. She read the clip and set it aside.

"You have a plan?" she asked. "Some particular way you want to organize this mess?"

I shook my head. I had no clear idea how to begin. "I thought I'd just start reading."

"If Marge was here we could have her build a database for you," Janet suggested. "We could input the key information from every story and have the computer cross-index everything."

I looked at her. "How long would that take?"

"Three or four days to input everything."

"We don't have that long," I told her.

She picked up the next piece of paper, read it, and set it aside. I did the same. She had started with the folder containing clips about the alderman so I started with the newspaper, reading every word of every story starting on page one and working my way back to the comics page. On page A8, filling the last few inches of a column next to a display ad for a shoe store, I found a brief story about Jerzy Hayden, a murdered wino who had finally been identified through dental records. I jotted his name in my notebook.

Nearly two hours later, as the last few minutes of the day were ticking away, she asked, "What was the name of the woman you introduced me to . . . the nurse?"

"Gleason," I said. "Sharon Gleason."

"Any connection?" She handed me two articles Bucky had written about a warehouse fire on September 7, 1957. The warehouse owned by Gleason Moving and Storage had burned to the ground shortly after 10 P.M., killing the owner, Holcomb Gleason. The police had suspected arson, but Bucky's follow-up story the next day said only that the fire had been declared an accident. Janet and I tore through the rest of Bucky's clips looking for additional information about the fire, but we found nothing. If Bucky had written Holcomb Gleason's obit, which was unlikely, it hadn't carried his byline so the intern I'd sent over to City

College wouldn't have known to copy it.

I made a note to myself to learn more about the fire and the subsequent investigation.

"About a month after this fire Kelvin was elected to the city council," Janet said, "and by the end of the year, it looks like Bucky was covering city hall on a regular basis. The last eleven stories with his byline that year were all about the council."

She showed the stories to me and I read over them. There were no startling revelations in any of them, hardly anything different than what I usually wrote. The most exciting clip concerned one alderman accusing another of being a "nigger lover."

In 1957.

Before the civil rights movement really got off the ground.

The accused turned out to be Kelvin.

9

WE DIDN'T FIND anything else of interest buried in the mountain of paper I'd brought home, and we finally called it a night. I was too tired to explore the treasures concealed by Janet's robe, and we fell asleep with her curled against my side, her warm breath tickling the hair on my chest.

The next morning I was slow to crawl out of bed, and didn't rouse until Janet carried a steaming mug of coffee into the bedroom and placed it on my nightstand.

"You'll be late," she said. "If you don't get up soon."

I crawled out of bed, downed the coffee before brushing my teeth, and staggered into the shower. I stood under the pulsing stream of scalding water and waited until the caffeine woke me before washing my hair, wincing only once when I forgot about the cut on my scalp and ran my fingers across it.

Janet was gone before I stepped out of the shower.

I toweled dry, pulled on my clothes, retrieved the clips about the Gleason warehouse fire, and drove directly to the newspaper. Once I arrived, I did three things: I called the kid from the morgue and told him I needed everything the paper had on the fire and related stories, as well as everything the paper Bucky had worked for had; asked Steven Harris to track down the original police reports regarding the fire; and opened up the telephone directory looking for Sharon Gleason's home phone number.

She wasn't listed.

A quick call to information also proved to be a dead-end, so I phoned the hospital where she worked. The personnel manager refused to provide information about the hospital's employees, even after I told her I was a newspaper reporter.

"I'm sorry, Mr. Fox," she said. "Hospital policy prevents me from providing that information to you over the phone. If you'd care to —"

"That's okay," I told her. "I'll just come down there myself."

Silverman was standing at my desk when I disconnected the line. "I saw your ugly mug on Channel 5 last night," he said. "The camera followed the casket down the steps of the cathedral and I saw the two of you standing there. Janet looked wonderful but you're not ready for prime time."

I had already pushed my chair back and was standing.

"You in a hurry?" he asked.

"Yeah, maybe," I told him. "I have a question I need answered."

"What's that?"

"Did you see the woman standing next to me, opposite side from Janet?"

"Briefly," Silverman said. "I wasn't paying attention to her."

"She keeps turning up and I need to talk to her. I don't know where she lives, but I know where she works. That's where I'm headed."

"Keep me posted," Silverman said.

"I always do," I told him.

On my way to the elevator, the kid from the morgue stopped me. He held a thin file folder containing our coverage of the 1957 Gleason Moving and Storage warehouse fire. I thumbed through everything and found Holcomb Gleason's obituary. He'd left behind a wife and an unnamed daughter.

I pulled the obit from the folder and pocketed it. I told the kid from the morgue to put everything else on my desk.

SHARON GLEASON SEEMED reluctant to speak with me when I found her in the children's burn ward at the hospital. "I have children to care for."

"This'll only take a few minutes," I said. I guided her into an empty waiting room. Then I asked her about the Alderman. "Why would he pay for your nursing school?"

"He said he owed it to my father."

"How did he know your father?"

"He never said. Neither did my mother."

"Your father was Holcomb Gleason? Died in a fire?"

"He was murdered."

I tapped my pen against my notebook.

"When did you first meet Kelvin?"

She shrugged. "I can't remember a time when I didn't know him."

"What would a lawyer and a guy with a moving and storage company have in common?"

"I really don't know," Gleason said. "May I go now?"

"What about your mother? Would she know the connection?"

"My mother passed on three years ago, God rest her soul." She glared at me. "You said this would only take a moment."

I took a deep breath and let it out slowly. I didn't know what else to ask, except for a way to contact her if I had any more questions.

She wrote her phone number in my notebook and then returned to her patients. I returned to the newspaper office.

"FINDING POLICE REPORTS from 1957 isn't a job for the weak," Steven Harris said as he dumped a pile of photocopies on my desk. "After I read these, I went to the courthouse and tracked down the trial records."

"Trial?" I pulled the copies toward me and began looking through them.

"The Gleason fire wasn't an accident," he explained. "It was arson."

That caught my attention and I looked up.

"The cops found a witness, guy named Jerzy Hayden."

I held up my hand to stop Harris and quickly thumbed through my notebook until I found Hayden's name. He was the wino killed three months earlier with the same gun used to kill Alderman Kelvin.

"The trial lasted less than a week and Tony Cooke was put away for life. His attorney didn't put up much of a defense."

It only took a moment of digging to learn that Anderson, Kline, and Myers had represented Cooke, and that William Kelvin had been the lead attorney.

"Where's Cooke now?" I asked.

Harris shrugged. "No one knows. He was released about six months ago, good behavior."

I phoned Detective Ballany and told him what I'd learned about Tony Cooke and the Gleason Moving and Storage fire.

"You think there's a connection between Cooke's release and the recent murders?" Ballany asked.

"There is a connection," I insisted. "Find Cooke and maybe he can explain what it is."

"He's reporting to a parole officer somewhere," Ballany said. "I'll see if I can find him."

Harris listened until I finally disconnected the line. "Anything else you need from me?" he said. "I have my own deadlines to meet."

Things were beginning to come together, but not in any way I had anticipated. I let Harris return to his own work, thanking him for tracking down the police file and court records. Then I took what I had into Silverman's office.

"So what's Bucky got to do with any of this?"

I pushed myself out of the office chair. "I'm working on it."

I PHONED JANET at her office and told her I wouldn't be home for dinner. She didn't seem to mind.

I only knew of two people who might remember Cooke's trial, the surviving original partners of Anderson, Kline, and Myers. I phoned the firm and learned that neither partner spent much time in the office.

Even though the receptionist wouldn't provide me with any personal information about the partners, it didn't take long for me to track down a home address.

I drove to Steve Anderson's house in Brentwood and leaned on the bell until he answered. After I identified myself, Anderson invited me in. I followed him to a plant-infested sunroom at the back of the house and was surprised to see Thomas Kline sitting in a deck chair.

"Thomas," Anderson said. "This is Mr. Fox. He's come to ask us a few questions."

Kline looked my way without recognition, and then returned his attention to the yard behind the house.

"He's only getting worse," Anderson said. "Before long, I won't be able to care for him myself."

Anderson wanted to talk, so I let him. He told me about Kline's condition, and how Alzheimer's had destroyed most of his short-term memory. "He doesn't even recognize people he's known for years," Anderson said. "I'm surprised he even remembers me."

I wanted to talk about Alderman Kelvin, the Gleason fire, and Cooke's trial. I waited until Anderson finished telling me how Kline had moved in after his wife's death.

"That was a long time ago," he said.

"1957."

Anderson hesitated so long I almost asked another question.

"You have to understand that things were different then," he finally said. "A lot different. A black man with a successful business was . . . unusual. St. Louis isn't the deep south, but we've had our share of problems over the years."

Kline's attention shifted from the back lawn to our conversation.

"A white man accused of killing a black man in 1957 wasn't going to get a fair trial, especially when the only witness was black."

"Are you saying Kelvin did something to ensure a guilty verdict?"

Anderson leaned forward. "William gave that man exactly the defense he deserved."

"But he was convicted."

"Rightly so," Anderson said. "Cooke was guilty. Only an all-white jury would think otherwise."

"So how —?"

"I told you times were different," Anderson explained. "The foreman of the jury was a cub reporter named Benjamin Weaver."

Bucky.

"He'd actually covered the original story, but that wasn't enough to disqualify him from the jury pool."

Kline started to smile, like he knew the punch line of a particularly funny joke.

"What would have disqualified him is something we discovered the day before trial began. His parents were high yellow."

"Bucky —"

"— was passing as white."

Kline started laughing, and laughing led to coughing. Anderson calmed his long-time partner and made him sip water.

"We let Benjamin know that we expected him to do the right thing. He convinced eleven white men to convict one of their own."

Before I left the two retired lawyers to their quiet study of the back lawn, I thanked them. When I left, Kline was still smiling.

BALLANY HAD PHONED while I was out, so I returned his call.

"Found Cooke," he said. "He's already confessed."

I didn't get the full story from Ballany until the next afternoon. We'd reserved a table at Greta's and he laid it all out for me.

"Jerzy Hayden was a coincidence," Ballany said. "Jerzy was panhandling about two blocks away from the restaurant where Cooke worked. Cooke recognized him and, on his way home one night, he popped Jerzy in back of the head. Then Cooke started thinking about the other people who had helped put him away."

As Ballany told it, Cooke had tracked down Kelvin and Weaver and had spent months learning their routines. The night he'd killed both men, Cooke had planned to shoot Bucky and put him in the car with Alderman Kelvin. His plans changed when Bucky staggered out of the bar. "He took advantage of the situation."

I thought about it for a moment and then asked, "Why did Kelvin call a payphone at the airport?"

"It wasn't a payphone," Ballany said. "It was one of those little kiosks, sells candy and magazines."

"Who'd he talk to?"

"Jerzy Hayden's granddaughter," Ballany explained. "She said the alderman saw something in the newspaper about her grandfather, and he phoned to express his regrets."

"He knew where Hayden's granddaughter was, but didn't know what had happened to Hayden?"

"The family says Hayden disappeared about ten years ago. Drinking took over his life and he said his family was better off without him. One day, he just walked out." Ballany took a drink. "The alderman had been helping the family ever since. He even helped the granddaughter get a job at the airport, put in a good word for her with the personnel department."

"What did Cooke expect to find in Bucky's apartment?"

Ballany shrugged. "He knew Bucky was foreman of the jury that convicted him. Cooke thought he could find something to prove that Bucky had colluded with the prosecution to sell him out. He claims there's no way a white jury would have convicted him."

I thought about what Steve Anderson had told me the previous day and wondered if Cooke might be correct. It certainly seemed unlikely that an all-white jury would have convicted Cooke in 1957, but he should have worried more about his defense team than the prosecution. I didn't tell Ballany that. I didn't tell Ballany anything I'd learned from Anderson.

★   ★   ★

I RETURNED TO the newspaper office after lunch and phoned the mayor. As soon as his secretary heard my name, she put me through to his honor.

"I know what ties Weaver and Alderman Kelvin together," I said. "The story will be in tomorrow's paper."

"You spoke to Steve Anderson yesterday," the mayor said. "I'm sure he said a few things that piqued your interest."

"Not a thing," I said. I had no reason to reveal the secret Bucky had kept his entire life. "He didn't tell me anything worth repeating."

The mayor hesitated, perhaps surprised by what I said. "That's good to hear, Fox," he said. "That's good to hear."

We ended the conversation a moment later, and then I turned to my computer and began writing. Someday I would be Benjamin "Bucky" Weaver, sitting in a bar, explaining to some snot-nosed kid how journalism seeps into your blood and into your bones, and how I'd once been some hot-shot, deadline-driven journalism machine, but not today.

Today, I have a deadline.

ABOUT THE AUTHOR

Michael Bracken is the author of 10 previous books, including *All White Girls, Bad Girls, Deadly Campaign, Psi Cops,* and *Tequila Sunrise*. Hundreds of his short stories have appeared in literary, small press, and commercial publications worldwide. He edits the *Fedora* series of hardboiled crime fiction anthologies and has edited a number of stand-alone mystery anthologies. He serves as vice president of the Mystery Writers of America's Southwest Chapter, president of the Short Mystery Fiction Society, and has served as chair of the Best First Novel committee for the Private Eye Writers of America's Shamus Awards.

Bracken received the Short Mystery Fiction Society's Derringer Award for "All My Yesterdays," and his story "Cuts Like a Knife" was short-listed for the Derringer Award. His non-fiction has appeared in numerous publications, and he has received many regional awards for advertising copywriting.

Additional information about Bracken is available at:
<www.CrimeFictionWriter.com>